"You were worth the wait."

Holly glanced over her shoulder as Clay helped her with her coat, but the lift of her eyebrows revealed more doubt than pleasure.

She had a warmth and a softness about her, but he sensed that circle of welcome didn't extend to everyone. Right now, she'd allowed him inside because of the night Santa had given to the kids she loved. But it would take more than that if he wanted to stay within that sphere.

If he wanted to....

He shouldn't even think about starting a relationship. Not now. Not when he had his family business to right.

But it's only one night.

"You look amazing," he said, reaching out to brush a tendril of hair back from her cheek.

Disbelief lingered in her gaze. She really didn't know how beautiful she was.

He was tempted to prove his words with a kiss....

Dear Reader,

Some dreams simply refuse to let go. They hang around no matter how impossible they seem or how many times you're tempted to give up on them. Writing has been a dream of mine for years, and I am thrilled to have my first book published by Silhouette Special Edition.

Like my dream of publishing, the characters of Holly and Clay refused to fade away. They first came to me in a short story I wrote for a community college writing course. I had a beginning, a middle and an end, but I knew there was so much more to these characters than the five pages I had given them! Years later, I took that same story and expanded it into the manuscript that became *All She Wants for Christmas*.

I hope you enjoy reading *All She Wants for Christmas,* and that Holly and Clay's story resonates for you like it has for me.

Happy holidays,

Stacy Connelly

ALL SHE WANTS
FOR CHRISTMAS

STACY CONNELLY

Silhouette

SPECIAL EDITION

Published by Silhouette Books

America's Publisher of Contemporary Romance

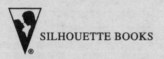

SILHOUETTE BOOKS

ISBN-13: 978-0-373-24944-2
ISBN-10:   0-373-24944-6

Recycling programs
for this product may
not exist in your area.

ALL SHE WANTS FOR CHRISTMAS

Books by Stacy Connelly

Silhouette Special Edition

All She Wants for Christmas #1944

STACY CONNELLY

has dreamed of publishing books since she was a kid, writing stories about a girl and her horse. Eventually, boys made it onto the page as she discovered a love of romance and the promise of happily-ever-after.

When she is not lost in the land of make-believe, Stacy lives in Arizona with her two spoiled dogs. Stacy loves to hear from her readers at stacyconnelly@cox.net.

Thank you to Susan Litman and Gail Chasan
for giving me this chance and for all the hard work
that went into my first book.

To the Loaded Pencils—
Karen, Dana, Teri, Pam and especially Betty
(for assigning the short story that eventually became
this book). Thanks for letting me be one of the "piñatas"
all these years.

To Kris—
For asking when my book was coming out
years and years before I was published!

To Kathy—
I'd need a whole book to list all the reasons why!

Chapter One

"Got some bad news, boss."

Clay Forrester looked up as his assistant ducked beneath the painter's scaffolding and played hopscotch over the electrical cords crisscrossing his office. Wallpaper swatches hung from a wall streaked with paint samples. Drop cloths protected his leather couch and chairs, but a fine layer of construction dust covered his mahogany desk. "What is it, Marie?"

Marie Cirillo opened her mouth just as the electrician started a high-powered drill. For a brief moment, the earsplitting electrical squeal seemed to emanate from his assistant. Clay choked back a laugh as she shot the construction worker an exasperated look.

The drilling stopped, and Clay asked, "Has anyone ever told you that you have a promising future as a ventriloquist's dummy?"

"You know, walking in here, I felt bad having to tell you this, but I'm feeling better about it now." She smirked. "Doug Frankle's sick."

His smile faded. "Our office Christmas party is in less than two hours, and our Santa is sick?"

The company party was being held two weeks before the holiday so it wouldn't interfere with family gatherings and vacations. The event was the culmination of a long, difficult year, and Clay was determined nothing would go wrong.

"Tell me we have a backup," he pleaded.

"His wife dropped off the costume if you want to substitute," Marie offered, with a cheeky grin.

Unfolding his six-foot frame from his leather chair, he ran a frustrated hand through his hair. "Do I look like a fat old man with a beard?"

"If Christmas was for the naughty instead of the nice, you're exactly what Santa Claus would look like."

"Very funny." Pulling out his wallet, Clay tossed two one-hundred-dollar bills onto his desk. "Go steal some supermarket Santa."

"You dare to bribe St. Nick?" Marie gasped in mock horror.

"Why not? Good ole St. Nick has been putting the thumbscrews to overworked parents for years. Accepting a bribe would be a step up from consumer extortion and emotional blackmail."

"You know, for a guy about to host a holiday party, you don't sound very festive." As the electrician left the office, mumbling something about splitters, she added, "You really haven't been yourself since—" She shut her mouth so quickly, her teeth clinked together. That his outspoken assistant even tried to curb her tongue was proof of her worry.

"Since my father died," he filled in for her. "You can say it, Marie."

She stepped closer. "You've changed, Clay. Back when your father was running the company—"

"He's not running the company anymore. *I* am."

Marie drew back slightly. "That's right. And you're doing

a damn good job. So don't you think it's time you start living in the present again?"

"What do you think I've been doing?"

"You're locked on the future and where you want the company to go, as if you can erase where it's been."

Clay flinched at the reminder of where the company had been—held tight within his father's hands. Only after Michael Forrester passed away had Clay realized how ruthless and relentless those hands could be.

"This is business, son," his father had once explained. "And business is all about the bottom line."

Growing up, Clay had accepted that statement, the same way he'd accepted that his father often missed the big game or the science fair, phoning in an excuse and leaving Clay and his sister to pretend to understand. It was business, after all, and business came first.

But not to everyone, Clay thought grimly as he recalled a confrontation several weeks after his father passed away. He'd been leaving for the day when an older man wearing a beat-up trench coat stopped him in the lobby. Taking one look at the man's bloodshot eyes and unkempt hair, Clay had assumed some bum had wandered in from the streets. Until the man called him by name.

"Where are your promises now, Forrester?" the man had demanded. "All the lies my grandchildren were foolish enough to believe about how you would 'turn the company around'? With a little more time, the loan would have come through, and *I* would have turned it around. But thanks to you, I never got the chance. You went behind my back, bought out the company from my own family and sold it off piece by piece until there was nothing left. *Nothing.*" His voice had broken on the word, and he'd pushed past Clay to rush out onto the sidewalk.

He hadn't tried to stop the man, hadn't said a thing. What was there to say? That time wouldn't have made a difference?

That no bank would give a struggling company a loan? That his father had been the one to decimate the man's business?

It was only later, on the long drive home, that Clay realized that he had no idea who the man was. That his business could have been any one of dozens.

Slowly, he was reversing the company's philosophy, from tearing down troubled companies to building them back up. His first move had been to give Kevin Hendrix, the CEO of Hendrix Properties, some practical business advice and infuse the company with capital, saving it from certain bankruptcy and assuring them both an impressive profit. He'd built on that success, certain he could change the company and his father's legacy.

"I'm trying to do what's right," Clay finally said to Marie. "And in case you've missed it, not everyone agrees."

Marie waved aside his comment. "Albert Jensen thinks only the bottom line counts."

Clay's smile twisted. "He wasn't my father's right-hand man for nothing." And while he didn't give a damn what Jensen thought, Clay couldn't escape the knowledge that his *father* would have disapproved.

Shaking off the dark thoughts, he said, "Look, no more business tonight. We've got a Christmas party to save. Go find someone to play Santa, and I promise to enjoy myself at the party."

"Sorry, Tiny Tim, but no can do," she responded.

"Oh, come on!" he exclaimed. "Don't tell me I've insulted your Christmas spirit."

Marie laughed. "Not quite. The caterers called. Their delivery truck broke down. I've got two dozen red-and-green cheesecakes to pick up."

"So it's a toss up between Santa and dessert?"

"Exactly. And I'm saving the cheesecake." She tossed the words over her shoulder as she strode from the office. "See you tonight." And then, as if to assure them both all was forgiven, she turned back, with a challenging glance. "And it better be in a red velvet suit."

You've changed, Clay. The accusation echoed in his mind long after Marie left. It was the same one Victoria had hurled at him the night she stormed out of their apartment—and out of their marriage.

She'd been furious that he'd missed some party. "I was working," he'd argued, the excuse uneasily familiar. And even though he and Victoria had lived like strangers for the last months of their relationship, at one time she'd known him very well. Well enough to make sure her pointed comments hit their mark.

"For a man so determined not to walk in his father's shoes, you're covering some well-worn ground."

As much as Clay wanted to argue, the proof was there—in the forgotten parties, the late dinners, the missed holidays.

Ever since the divorce, he'd kept his life simple, with no one to disappoint, no one to let down. No one…

The office door opened again, interrupting his thoughts. The electrician reentered, toolbox and several wires in hand. "Sorry to disturb you, Mr. Forrester."

The office remodeling had taken so long, Clay had grown accustomed to the ever-present construction workers. With a sigh of frustration, he asked, "I don't suppose you know where I can find a Santa Claus?" Hearing how stupid he sounded, he vowed he would fire the electrician on the spot if the man said "The North Pole."

Setting his toolbox on the floor, the man said, "There's been a Santa in the lobby all week. In front of that flower shop."

"You're kidding." Clay walked by the flower shop on his way to the elevator every day. How had he missed a fat man in a velvet suit? Maybe Marie was right. He had focused too much on work lately. He glanced at his watch. Floral Fascinations closed at six. He still had a few minutes. "Thanks for the tip." Grabbing his jacket from the back of his chair, he said, "Are you almost finished for today?"

"I'll be done in a few minutes." A shower of sparks flared from the Christmas-colored wires. Clay shook his head and left his office, with the man's curses following him out the door.

The reception area was empty. Marie was already en route to rescue the stranded cheesecakes. A small stack of files lined the edge of her otherwise bare desk. For all her teasing remarks, she was an amazing assistant. He couldn't have managed this last year without her. No doubt the files were ones he needed first thing Monday morning.

As Clay stepped inside the elevator car, he vowed to put work aside. He needed a night to relax, and the party promised to be a good time. He'd invited the employees to the elegant Lakeshore Plaza Hotel ballroom. He had caterers and a band lined up, gifts to raffle. All he needed was a substitute Santa.

Moments later, the elevator bell chimed, and the doors slid open to reveal the elegant gray and white marble lobby. Green garlands trailed down either side of the black granite water feature. Red bows and mistletoe decorated the floor-to-ceiling marble columns. Piped-in music played Christmas carols.

And, sure enough, a red-suited St. Nick stood outside the flower shop. After a quick greeting, Clay cut to the bottom line. "I have a holiday party tonight and a sick Santa. How about a hundred dollars to fill in?"

He pulled the money from his wallet and watched the man's eyes widen above his snowy beard. Looking far more greedy than jolly, the man protested, "I already got another gig lined up."

Recognizing the negotiating tactic, Clay pulled a second bill from his wallet. "Does it pay two hundred dollars and include a meal catered by one of Chicago's finest restaurants?"

Santa snatched the money from Clay's hand.

* * *

Holly Bainbridge flipped the hanging sign to Closed, slipped out of the flower shop, and locked the door behind her. Six o'clock. She had a half an hour to get to the foster home. Pocketing the keys, she turned and was surprised to see Clay Forrester talking to the storefront Santa.

Working in the same building as Forrester Industries, even if it was thirty some floors below his skyscraping offices, Holly knew his company's reputation as an avaricious giant, gobbling up small businesses. And she'd seen for herself how ruthless Clay Forrester could be. Months ago, she'd watched, unnoticed, as he stared down some poor old man whose company he had destroyed. Forrester hadn't bothered to say a single word; his features—and his heart—could have been carved from the same stone that filled the lobby.

Holly had dealt with that kind of ruthlessness before, with the kind of hardball businessmen who cared more about turning a profit than turning foster children out of their home. Fury filled her, but Holly buried the useless emotion and the ache of tears that accompanied it.

She watched Forrester hand the Santa a piece of paper. Was he donating to charity? Perhaps the holiday spirit had the power to touch even the most cynical hearts. Forrester smiled, but the twitch of his lips reflected the look of a man who accepted victory as his due.

Holly waited until he strode away before approaching. "We'll have to hurry to get there on time, Charlie," she told the costumed Santa.

A bad feeling crept into her stomach the second he glanced toward Clay Forrester's departing figure. "Uh, Miss Bainbridge, something's come up. I've got another party to go to."

She couldn't believe it. "I have half a dozen kids waiting for Santa, and you're going to disappoint them?"

"Sorry, Miss Bainbridge."

Sorry. People always said they were sorry. But apologies didn't make heartaches heal any faster or hurt any less. She had promised the foster kids at Hopewell House a Santa, and she was not going to disappoint them! Especially *this* year, when the group home would soon be closing its doors for good.

Determined, Holly marched toward the elevators where Clay Forrester stood waiting. A bell chimed, and the gilded mirrored doors slid open. The rapid tattoo of her boots striking the marble floors increased as she ran toward the elevator. She squeezed through the doors, with inches to spare.

He glanced at her with a touch of curiosity as the elevator rose. Holly had seen the handsome businessman before; a woman would have to be blind not to notice six feet of black-haired, blue-eyed perfection. But she'd never had the chance to study him up close. Never noticed the straight, serious eyebrows, the stubborn jaw, his sculpted, sensuous mouth…

"Mr. Forrester…" Flustered by the huskiness in her voice, Holly stopped speaking.

He looked again, charting a course from the top of her dark hair, to her sweater and jeans, to her ankle boots. By the time his lingering gaze made its way back to hers, curiosity had turned to interest, and somehow the elevator reached high enough altitude to steal the breath from Holly's lungs.

"I'm sorry. Do I know you?"

It should have put her at an advantage, knowing who he was when he didn't know her. Instead, Holly felt insignificant. "Holly Bainbridge. I work at the flower shop, and you stole my Santa."

"Excuse me?"

She flushed. If only he weren't so darn good-looking, maybe she could complete an intelligent sentence. "Charlie promised me he would make an appearance tonight."

"He did mention another job, but—"

His words cut off as the elevator jerked to an abrupt halt. Holly gasped, losing her balance and falling against Clay. He caught her body with his as the elevator went dark. She couldn't see a thing.

But she could feel. Oh, yes, she could *feel*. The imprint of each finger grasping her upper arms. The slight catch in his breath as her breasts grazed his chest, the quickening of his heartbeat. His rock-solid chest beneath her hands. And his belt buckle, hard and cold against her stomach, a sharp contrast to the rest of him, which was definitely hard and warm.

Awareness skittered along nerve endings, and her own heart beat double time, nearly drowning out the sound of their combined breathing.

"What happened?" she asked when she found her voice.

Holly felt the slight shaking of his chest a split second before laughter filled the small space. Jerking away, she demanded, "What's so funny?"

"I've got the Three Stooges remodeling my office, and my guess is that Larry just blew a fuse."

Adrift in the darkness, without his touch to anchor her, she reached back for the elevator wall. "The building's lost power?"

"With the luck I've had recently," he said wryly, "all Chicago's probably lost power."

A faint electronic hum punctuated his words, and after a tense moment hanging in space, the car resumed its ascent. Giving a sigh of relief, Holly closed her eyes and sank against the side of the car.

"Are you okay?"

Opening her eyes to find Clay standing inches away, Holly thought the elevator might have fallen after all. She certainly felt like she'd lost touch with solid ground, her heart hovering somewhere in her throat. She grasped hold of the handrail to keep from swaying closer. "I'm—I'm fine."

He searched her expression as if looking for the truth, and Holly purposefully held his gaze instead of allowing her attention to slip to his lips, hovering above her own.

In a voice deeper than moments before, Clay said, "I'm sorry about the Santa thing."

His words dimmed the rush of attraction as Holly imagined using that brush off with the disappointed children. *Hey, kids, sorry about the Santa thing.*

The casual crushing of hopes and dreams reminded her of her ex-boyfriend's easy defection. Even after she'd trusted Mark enough to share the truth about her painful childhood, he'd let her down in the worst possible way. "Sorry, Holly, but I don't even know if I want kids of my own, let alone raise someone else's kid."

Those words, spoken by the man she thought she loved, the man she thought she wanted to marry, had instantly dragged her into the past. Into her old insecurities about her self-worth.

She wasn't like other people. She didn't have biological ties to bind her to another living soul. She wasn't Bob and Carol's daughter or Jimmy's little sister.

Holly had truly thought she'd escaped those stigmas, until Mark's insensitive remark brought them all back. Now she couldn't escape the fear that her rootless past might haunt her yet again. What if the system decided a nobody like her wasn't good enough to be a foster mother?

"Look, maybe there's something I can do," Clay offered.

It took a second for Holly to refocus on the conversation and realize he was talking about the Santa-less Christmas party. "I don't know what," she said, not putting much hope in the offer as the elevator bell announced their arrival at the top floor.

"Let's call Charlie."

Slipping through the doors the moment they opened, Clay didn't look back as his long strides carried him into the reception area. Completely focused on what he wanted, he didn't wait to see if she followed. Holly gazed at the button for the lobby. It would be so easy to push the button and slip away from Clay Forrester, hopefully leaving her disconcerting attraction behind....

"I don't have his number," she said as she stepped off the elevator and into the plush office. Her heels sank into the patterned carpet, and she glanced at the leather chairs and a circular work-station. Double doors barred the way to Clay's inner sanctum.

"Okay." Her words barely slowed his stride. "I'll call the hotel where my party's being held and tell Charlie to go to yours instead."

His determination knocked the legs out from under her earlier anger. After all, Charlie was the one who'd broken his promise, but Holly couldn't forget that Clay's money had been the deciding factor. As always, money talked, and Holly went through life unheard.

"What time does your party start?" she asked.

Clay twisted his wrist to check his watch, and Holly caught a glimpse of gold and the expensive wink of diamonds. "In an hour and a half."

An hour and a half before they could reach Charlie—if he showed on time—then the ride from the hotel to Hopewell House… Holly shook her head. "That would be too late."

The children at Hopewell House were no strangers to dis-appointment, a feeling Holly recalled all too well from her own childhood. But how she had wanted their last Christmas together to be one to remember!

"Too late?" Clay echoed. "Where are you supposed to be tonight?"

"At a party at Hopewell House."

"What's that?"

"It's a group home for foster children."

He stared at her. "You mean to tell me that I stole Santa Claus from a bunch of foster kids?" Regret etched a line between his eyebrows as he sank back against the reception desk, and Holly had the odd desire to make *him* feel better.

"I'll think of something."

Maybe the two women who ran the group home had kept

Santa's arrival a secret. Perhaps she could arrange for a different Santa to entertain the kids. It would have to be soon, though, before the children were separated and placed in new homes. Before Hopewell House closed forever.

She was turning to leave when Clay called out, "Wait."

He caught her hand for a brief second, and a tingle of warmth shot up her arm, even after she pulled her hand from his grasp. Holly longed to wipe her palm against her jeans to dull the sensation. But the sudden intensity in his blue eyes indicated he'd experienced the same flare of attraction. Her mouth suddenly went dry, and she couldn't look away, the sexual connection far harder to break than the physical one.

"Miss Bain…Holly," he hesitated. "If there's anything I can do…"

She shook her head. "I don't know how much it cost you to buy my Santa, but this isn't a problem money can solve."

Holly pulled her beat-up Volkswagen Bug to a stop in front of Hopewell House. Looking at the house, with its cheery Christmas lights and welcoming glow, she took a deep breath.

Normally, she loved volunteering at the group home. With the impending closure, she'd spent every spare moment inside its warm, loving walls. The children never failed to lift her spirits, but tonight she dreaded the thought of entering the two-story brownstone.

After leaving Clay in his office, Holly had gone back to the flower shop. She'd worked her way through the directory listings for costume shops. Most of her calls had gone straight through to voice mail; those that had been answered had ended in disappointment, with all the Santa suits already rented.

Her breath began to fog the windows, and Holly couldn't put it off any longer. Bundled up against the chilly Chicago night, she climbed from the car, slammed the door, and ran up the walkway to the steps.

The second she set foot on the porch, the front door opened, and Eleanor Hopewell waved her plump hands, urging her inside. "Come in! Come in! You'll catch your death."

The sixty-something woman gathered Holly's knitted scarf and jacket and hung them on waist-high, bright plastic hooks. "The children are so excited!" Eleanor's faded blue eyes sparkled behind her glasses.

Holly held back a groan. "Eleanor—"

Before Holly had the chance to break the bad news, Eleanor's sister, Sylvia, bustled into the foyer. "What are you doing keeping Holly in the doorway? Bring her into the parlor! Mary Jane can't wait for you to hear her songs!"

Flanked by the two women, Holly dragged her feet but still wound up in the parlor. A half a dozen kids, ranging in age from three to seven, looked up as she entered.

"Holly, do you want to hear 'Frosty the Snowman' or 'Twinkle, Twinkle Little Star'?" Mary Jane called out, her small hands poised above the piano's keys.

"That's not a Christmas song!" a know-it-all voice shouted.

"Is too!" Mary Jane argued. "'Cause there's a star on top of the tree."

"Miss Holly?" Holly felt a tug at her sweater and looked down. Bright blue eyes stared up at her from beneath a fringe of blond bangs. She knelt down until she was face-to-face with the three-year-old boy. Longing and hope rushed through her. Would she be given the chance to adopt Lucas? To be more than Miss Holly to this little boy she adored? "Hi, Lucas."

A look of concern crossed his face. "How can San'a come down the chi'ney now?"

Holly followed the chubby finger he pointed toward the fire-place. Homemade stockings hung from the mantle, and a cheery fire blazed in the hearth. The mention of Santa sent disappointment surging through her. "Lucas, about Santa—"

Eleanor interrupted before Holly could break the news.

"Now, Lucas, don't worry. Santa Claus has to be very clever to get toys to all the good boys and girls. He'll figure out something."

Eleanor had no more than said the words when the doorbell rang. The children and the two older women gasped in anticipation. Mary Jane jumped up from the piano. "It's Santa!"

"No, wait." The stampede of tiny shoes pounding the wood floors drowned out Holly's protest. The weight of disappointing the children pressed down on her, and she sank into a chair, not bothering to follow everyone to the foyer.

Holly heard the front door open and Eleanor's exclamation, "Children, look who's here!"

Cries of "Santa!" combined with a deep belly laugh. "Ho-ho-ho! Merry Christmas!"

Holly jumped up. Was it possible? Had Charlie changed his mind? Amazed, she walked to the doorway and watched as Eleanor and Sylvia introduced the children one by one to the bearded man in the red velvet suit. The children gazed up in adoration. Santa spoke to each child in turn, calling them by name and tousling their hair.

Holly frowned. After nearly two weeks in front of the flower shop, Charlie rarely remembered *her* name. How was it that he suddenly recalled the names of half a dozen children?

When it came to Lucas's turn, he took one look at the white-haired, overstuffed man and ran in the opposite direction. As the little boy took refuge behind Holly's legs, Santa glanced her way for the first time.

Holly barely kept an astounded gasp from escaping as she looked into Clay Forrester's unmistakable blue eyes.

Chapter Two

Stunned, her heart pounding, Holly could only stare. With Clay decked out in full Santa regalia and surrounded by children, the scene looked like a Christmas card come to life.

As long as no one looked too closely at the flirtatious gleam in his eyes or the sexy smile the fake beard and mustache failed to hide.

"Come on, Lucas," Eleanor Hopewell encouraged. "Come meet Santa. You've been so excited all week."

Lucas tightened his arms on Holly's legs, and Holly felt just as reluctant to approach the man in the red velvet suit. Unfortunately, she had no one to hide behind, and both Eleanor and Clay were waiting. Eleanor, with her hands clasped together in excited anticipation; Clay, with one bushy white eyebrow arched in challenge.

Taking a deep breath, Holly reached for the boy's hand and squeezed reassuringly. "Let's go, Lucas."

Lucas stayed mostly hidden behind one of her legs, but she coaxed him out long enough for him to mouth a silent "Hi."

Then, as if Holly were one of the children, Eleanor said, "Santa, this is Holly."

"Well, hello, Holly." Clay's eyes sparkled. "Come give Santa a hug."

With all eyes focused on them, she had no choice but to step forward. Clay immediately wrapped his arms around her in an exaggerated embrace. She stumbled against him, but thanks to the pillow stuffed inside the velvet jacket, she was saved the body contact that had robbed her breath in the elevator.

Even so, his hands found the thin strip of bare skin where her sweater pulled away from her waistband. Had she really thought of him as being cold? Heat emanated from his touch, and a small shiver raced through her. His fake beard tickled her nose, and the enticing hint of his aftershave made Holly desperate to create some space between them. Or bury her nose deeper to search out more of the scent on his skin.

"Mr.…Claus, please!" she protested.

"Tell me, Holly—" his deep murmur sent another shiver down her spine "—have you been naughty or nice?" With that rakish lift of one eyebrow, he flashed a *very* naughty grin.

She managed a flustered smile and said, "I've been good."

"Thought so." He winked. "I can always tell."

He let her go, and Holly took a grateful step back, wondering how the parlor fireplace managed to give off so much heat in the foyer.

"Santa Claus, do you want to hear me play 'Frosty the Snowman'?" Mary Jane asked.

"In a minute, my dear. Wait while my little helper—" he grabbed Holly's hand "—and I bring in a surprise for all of you."

"Don't forget your coat." Sylvia draped the jacket around Holly's shoulders, and before Holly knew what had happened, she found herself outside, alone, with Clay Forrester.

The scent of snow tinged the air, along with a hint of chimney smoke drifting in the night sky. The street was silent and still, breathless with anticipation. It was only as she had to suck in a quick breath that Holly realized *she* was the one who'd forgotten to breathe. "What... How—"

Ignoring her stumbling words, Clay pushed the hat back far enough for his dark hair to fall over his forehead. He blew a cloud of air upward, ruffling his bangs. "You wouldn't believe how hot this costume is."

Gathering her wits and the edges of her jacket together, she asked, "How did you know where to find me?"

"You told me you were coming to Hopewell House." He gestured to the brass placard near the front door.

Holly stepped back and took in the sight of the successful businessman in his full St. Nick glory. She still couldn't believe her eyes. "Where on earth did you get that costume? I called all over and couldn't find one."

Looking uncomfortable, he confessed, "I already had it."

Holly frowned. "If you *had* the costume, why'd you need Charlie?"

"I had the *costume.* I didn't have anyone to wear it. No way was I going to make a fool of myself dressing like Santa at my company party."

"But you're here." She waved a hand, gesturing to the costume and Hopewell House, glowing brightly behind them.

"Yeah, I am."

Holly told herself not to read too much into his words, but how could she miss what his actions were saying? He'd been willing to make a fool of himself to do her a favor....

Swallowing, she tried to lighten the moment with a nod to the black limo waiting by the curb. "What happened to the sleigh and reindeer?" she asked as the two of them walked toward the car.

"Traded them in for four hundred horses." He waved at the

driver, who was hidden behind the tinted windows, and the trunk popped open.

The uniformed driver climbed from the limo. "Need any help with that, sir?"

"We've got it, Roger. Thanks." Clay pushed the trunk open all the way.

If his arrival had shocked her speechless, the sight of the overloaded bags of toys sent words spilling from her mouth. "Look at all… Where did you… *How* did you have time to buy all this?"

"I had some help," he confessed.

With a laugh shaky enough to reveal the tears she was trying not to cry, she asked, "Elves?"

"Close. Personal shopper." His knowing gaze caught hers as he pulled out the first bag and passed it to her. "I thought about what you said and decided you were right. There are problems money can't solve, but there are times when it works miracles."

Heated embarrassment rushed to her face. "Mr. Forrester—"

"I think you can call me Clay." He grabbed the other two bags of toys and closed the trunk.

"I'm sorry about what I said back at your office," she told him as they walked back toward the house.

"You were right." He slanted her a glance. "Don't apologize."

But she'd been wrong. Had anyone asked that morning, Holly would have sworn the successful businessman cared only about profit margins and saw people in terms of black and red: what they contributed in comparison to what they cost.

After their elevator mishap, she had thought perhaps she'd misjudged him but hadn't expected him to give a second thought to the children waiting for a Christmas that might not come. Yet he'd taken time away from his own party to show up and play Santa. She felt as giddy and amazed as the children waiting inside.

Clay started to walk through the front door, but Holly grabbed his arm. "Wait."

Setting her bag on the porch, she reached up, straightened the hat he'd pushed back, and carefully smoothed his dark hair beneath the white trim. Only when his surprised gaze locked with hers did she realized what she'd done. Stepping back, Holly cleared her throat. "Can't have the kids figuring out you're not really Santa."

He reached up to adjust the hat, and she turned away, grateful to escape before doing something even more foolish. She opened the front door, and together they walked back to the parlor.

"Now, children, step back! Give Santa some room to breathe!" Sylvia admonished the kids who danced around him as they tried to peek inside the bags he carried.

Clay purposely lowered the bags to give the children a glimpse of gleaming tow trucks, blocks, and dolls before lifting them out of sight once more. Bobbing up and down on tiptoe, Mary Jane turned to the little girl beside her. "I saw a Barbie doll!"

Clay must have heard the exaggerated whisper. Once he settled into the parlor's wingback chair, the fireplace and Christmas tree on either side, he motioned the two girls forward and pulled out a Barbie for each of them. Their eyes bright with excitement, they had the boxes open and were exchanging accessories within minutes.

The children's happiness was contagious, and Eleanor and Sylvia seemed just as excited. Clay's belly laugh filled the cozy room, and the blue eyes that had given him away in the first place danced.

If Holly had taken the job of matching the toys up with the children, she couldn't have done better. Some, like Mary Jane, were easy, but for shy toddlers like Lucas, picking the perfect toy was more difficult. And even then, Holly couldn't fault Clay's choice.

Prompted by Holly, Lucas ran over just long enough to grab the yellow fire truck Clay held out. Holly tried to show Lucas how the battery-operated vehicle worked, but he wouldn't let go of the toy to set it motoring across the floor.

As Eleanor walked toward the kitchen for refills of the fragrant, steaming cider, she stopped at Holly's side. "That man is a wonder," the older woman whispered. "When he called for directions, he asked about the children's Christmas lists, but I never expected this."

So that was how Clay had known what to buy. The knowledge didn't lessen Holly's amazement. She was touched he'd thought to research which presents would mean the most to the children. "I never expected it, either."

"Wherever did he come from?" Eleanor asked.

Still awed that Clay Forrester was playing Santa for their party, Holly shook her head and mumbled, "Fortune 500."

"Excuse me, dear?"

"I said I was fortunate to find him."

He picked that moment to glance her way, and the distance separating them did little to dim the effect his appraising gaze had on her. The rest of the room faded away, leaving only the two of them.

Dressed in the Santa Claus suit, he should have looked silly. Sweet, at best. So how was it that she found him every bit as sexy as when she'd seen him in his designer suit?

"I can see how this might turn out very fortunate, indeed," Eleanor said, with a delighted chuckle.

The older lady's thoughts weren't hard to follow, but Holly shook her head. "It's not what you think."

"This isn't about what I think. This is about facts. Like the fact that your Mr. Forrester is the first man you've ever invited here."

"He isn't the first man I've invited," Holly refuted softly. "He's just the first to actually show."

She'd asked Mark to visit the group home with her several

times while they were dating, hoping to ease him into the idea of fostering Lucas. But there'd been nothing easy about it.

At first glance, Mark had been everything a woman hoped for: handsome, smart, charming. Only later did Holly realize he'd been playing a part to get what he wanted. Before long, their entire relationship was based on his needs.

And one thing he hadn't wanted was to even consider the possibility of raising *someone else's kid*.

But it didn't matter whether or not Clay was anything like Mark. Clay Forrester had a pedigreed family history; Holly had never even found out who her parents were.

The differences that started at birth had continued throughout their lives. He was the CEO of a multimillion-dollar company; she struggled to make ends meet working at a flower shop. He was champagne and caviar. She was soda pop and tuna fish. A chauffeur-driven limousine compared to a VW Bug.

And Holly knew better than to fantasize that any of those things mixed, no matter what Eleanor thought.

Clay hadn't sung Christmas carols in years, but even he knew Mary Jane and her fellow singers were a good octave off. Standing beside the piano, having been given the important job of page turning while Mary Jane played, he couldn't help smiling. Traditions that had gotten lost in overcommercialization came back to life in the children's happiness.

If Marie could see me now. He'd meant what he said to Holly. No way would he have put on the costume and made a fool of himself in front of his employees. But the second he'd seen the disappointment in Holly's eyes, he'd known he was going to make a fool of himself, after all. All for a woman whose mysterious green gaze quickened his heartbeat.

Not that he'd jumped at the chance to play Santa. He'd spent a good ten minutes pacing his office, trying to convince himself he wasn't at fault. But the excuse rang hollow.

Because even though he hadn't known Charlie was headed to the foster home, the man *had* said he was booked for another job, and instead of accepting that, Clay had negotiated a deal where he came out the winner, loser be damned. He hadn't thought twice about making Charlie a better offer, and if not for Holly, he wouldn't have thought about it at all.

So he'd donned the Santa outfit to salvage Christmas and his conscience, totally ignoring the mocking voice that laughed over the stupid things a man would do for a beautiful woman.

"Wonderful job, children," Sylvia complimented, her clapping signaling an end to the sing-along before Mary Jane could launch into yet another round of "Frosty the Snowman." Holding up a camera, she said, "How about a picture with Santa?"

Seated once more in the parlor chair, Clay posed with each child on his knee while Sylvia coaxed them to say "Cheese." As he held Lucas on his lap, with the little boy tugging on his beard, Clay noticed Holly watching. For a brief second, he thought he saw tears in her eyes, but then the flash blinded him. She was smiling by the time she bent to lift Lucas from his lap.

She straightened and perched Lucas on one hip, but the little boy swung his booted feet, a silent demand to get down. The minute Holly released him, Lucas dropped to his knees and was off, pushing his fire truck across the braided rug.

Clay caught her wrist, claiming her attention with a slight tug. He ran his thumb across the back of her hand and smiled when her pulse leaped beneath his fingers. Thoughts of discovering even smoother skin and more intimate pulse points sent his own blood pumping.

"Come on, Holly. Don't you have any Christmas wishes?"

The color in her cheeks brightened as she tucked her dark hair behind one ear. Despite the uncertainty in her green eyes, her tone of voice was composed and dry as she said, "I'll drop a letter to the North Pole."

He shook his head, careful not to dislodge the hat and white wig. "It works better in person. So tell me. There must be something you want."

Despite the teasing question, Clay hoped for a serious answer. He wanted to know about Holly. She was different from Victoria. So selfless and giving.

Oh, he knew plenty of people, himself included, who made donations this time of year. He wrote checks for numerous charities, but Holly obviously did more than give money. She gave a part of herself.

He sensed she was the kind of person who never put her head before her heart. A woman who led with her feelings, accepting the risk of ending up emotionally bruised. But as much as Clay admired her for that, he'd learned his lesson when it came to leaving his heart unprotected. Some risks weren't worth repeating.

As Holly gently tugged her hand from his, her gaze sought out Lucas. Keeping her voice a low murmur, she said, "I'm sorry, Clay, but I don't believe in Santa Claus."

"Miss Holly! You're doing it *wrong*." Mary Jane's exasperated voice rose above the parlor's cheerful din. "You're supposed to sit on Santa's lap."

"That's just for boys and girls," Holly answered quickly, with a reproachful glance at Clay, as if disapproving of whatever he might say. "It's different for grown-ups."

Her narrowed gaze expressed her doubt, but the little girl said, "But you still get your wish, right?"

"Well?" Clay prompted, knowing Mary Jane had Holly trapped. "There must be some long-ago wish Santa never granted you as a child."

Emotions flickered across her expression, and longing filled her green eyes. In that moment, Clay vowed that anything she wanted, anything she asked for, he would give her.

"Holly—"

"A pony," Holly blurted out. Her forced smile couldn't erase the shadow from her eyes as she turned to Mary Jane. "Don't all little girls ask for ponies?"

"Barbie has a pony," Mary Jane added, with a not-so-subtle look at Santa.

"Then a pony it is," Clay agreed, realizing his own wish to get to know Holly better was going to go unanswered. At least for now.

After another round of pictures, including ones of Eleanor and Sylvia, Clay had the feeling he was overstaying the kids' bedtime. Earlier, Lucas had climbed into Holly's arms and fallen asleep, his fire truck cradled against his chest and her cheek pressed to the top of his head. When she'd caught Clay watching, she gently pried the truck from Lucas's hands and stood, carrying the little boy from the parlor as the Hopewell sisters rounded up the older kids to brush their teeth.

He should say good-night. He'd done what he'd come to do, and his employees were waiting for him at the party. Even though he'd called Marie to tell her he'd be late, she wouldn't be able to cover for him for long.

He should go.

Pushing to his feet, Clay eyed the front door, then the hallway where Holly had disappeared. The hall light gleamed, but the sound of her voice guided him. Singing "Silent Night," her soft, sweet voice called to him like a siren. Standing in the doorway, he watched, unseen.

Holly sat on the small bed. Leaning forward, she brushed Lucas's hair back and pressed a kiss to the sleeping boy's forehead. Every gesture spoke of caring and compassion. Volunteering at the foster home clearly wasn't something she did out of duty or responsibility. She did it for love.

His fingers itched to sink into Holly's hair as he pressed his lips to hers and...well, to do more than simply tuck *her* into bed.

The surge of desire took him by surprise. After watching Holly all evening, he knew she wasn't his type. She had home and family written on her soul. He had a divorce in his past and a business to run in his future. No woman would settle for what little he could offer. Victoria certainly hadn't, not when there were men who could offer so much more.

He'd already lost his marriage to the company his father had started. No point in trying and losing again. At least, not as long as business was his main focus and his nemesis, Albert Jensen, fought to block his every move.

He'd made up his mind that it was time to go when Holly looked up. She pressed a finger to her lips, warning him to be quiet, but there was little chance of him speaking. He couldn't get a word past his suddenly dry throat as he stared at her mouth.

She would taste sweet, like the candy canes hanging from the Christmas tree, but with a hint of spice from the hot cider she'd drunk earlier. Most of all, though, she would taste like soft, warm woman, and it was all Clay could do not to pull her into his arms when she brushed by him in the doorway.

She eased the door shut and whispered, "He's out like a light. Probably dreaming of fire trucks and reindeer." Her sweet smile revealed she didn't have a clue as to the hungry, heated thoughts tempting him.

Clay lifted a hand toward her face and caught sight of the white-trimmed cuff attached to the red velvet sleeve. No wonder Holly had no idea what he was thinking. There was something just plain *wrong* about Santa Claus making moves on a woman!

But he couldn't bring himself to lower his hand without brushing Holly's hair back from her shoulder. The silken strands teased his knuckles, adding to his torment as he imagined her hair brushing against his face, his chest.

Damn, he really needed to go. Now.

Keeping her voice low as she led the way back to the parlor,

Holly said, "I don't think I've ever seen the kids so happy. You've made this their best Christmas ever."

With the Hopewell sisters settling the older children into bed, the parlor was empty. The fire had died down, and the piano was silent.

"I'll walk you out," Holly offered. She bundled up once more and followed him to the front porch. The outside light cast a golden glow around her, adding to her innocent aura. "I don't know how to thank you for everything you did."

Clay was starting to brush off her gratitude when an idea came to him, overriding his earlier vows. After all, it was just a few more hours, and if Holly really wanted to pay him back, he knew the perfect way.

"Funny you should mention that," he said. "I know just how you can thank me." He read the surprise on her face and laughed. "Shame on you, Miss Bainbridge. My intentions are completely honorable." When she still gave him a doubtful look, he held his hands out to his sides. "If you can't trust Santa Claus—"

Her lips tilted in a hint of a smile, which faded just as quickly. "I don't know how I could possibly repay you."

"Come with me tonight."

"What?" Her eyes widened at the impulsive request, and he could read the hesitation written there. If that were all he'd seen, he would have let it go. But he'd also noticed a spark that told him his attraction wasn't one-sided.

As he stepped closer, he felt the blood in his veins heat up as he watched that spark flare a little bit brighter. Pulling off the hat and beard that covered his face, he said, "I'm asking you to be my date at my party."

Chapter Three

Shocked, Holly protested. "I don't know anything about corporate parties!"

"It'll be like this one, only with alcohol and worse manners." He shrugged. "Besides, I went to your party."

"I wouldn't have needed you to come to my party if you hadn't stolen my Santa."

His hand cut through the chill night air, dismissing her argument. "Details."

Holly ducked her head. The thought of trying to fit in at a party filled with wealthy, successful businessmen and women sent her into a panic. The idea was preposterous, but not nearly as preposterous as Clay showing up dressed as Santa Claus.

"All right," she agreed slowly. She looked down at the red sweater and black jeans she wore. "But I'll have to stop by my apartment to change clothes."

"Yeah." Clay hooked his thumbs into the wide black belt circling his enlarged stomach. "Me, too. I knew I'd be pressed for time, so I brought clothes along. If I change at your place, my driver can take us to the party together."

She didn't live far, and Holly certainly didn't want to arrive at the party alone. "Okay. Do you want to follow me?"

"Roger can follow. I'll ride with you."

After Clay notified the driver of their plans, he joined Holly in her car. She chuckled when he unbuttoned the red jacket and pulled out the pillow he'd used for stuffing. As she drove, she glanced at Clay, catching glimpses of his profile in the passing streetlights. "What's the party going to be like?"

"Well, I know we'll have cheesecake." His teeth flashed in the shifting light. "Music, dancing. This year has been… Well, it's been a transition of sorts." His voice sounded tight, different from his usual teasing tone. "I hope the party will bring everyone together."

Holly parked her car in front of her apartment building, the limo behind her. After retrieving a black garment bag from Roger, Clay and Holly walked up the steps to the five-story, redbrick building, the winter wind pushing them forward. Holly drew her keys out of her purse, but the key ring slipped from her cold fingers. She bent down, but Clay was faster, and her fingers tangled with his. Unlike her own icy hand, his was warm, and she didn't want to pull away.

His gaze captured hers, the keys forgotten. Their breath mingled in the night air, but Holly no longer noticed the chill. As he helped her up, the warmth seeped even deeper, weakening her knees. He unlocked the door and handed her the keys once they stepped inside the foyer.

As they took the stairs to the third floor, Holly tried to remember if she'd left laundry piled on the couch or fast-food wrappers on the table. Opening the door, she flicked on the light and breathed a sigh of relief. Only a pair of discarded shoes cluttered the living room.

Holly sensed more than she saw Clay evaluating the apartment. It had come furnished with well-worn, utilitarian furniture. The beige couch and chair matched the walls and carpet. She supposed her place looked like every other apartment in the building.

She pointed to the bathroom and said, "You can change in there."

Holding up the hat he'd pulled off back at Hopewell House, he raised a bushy white eyebrow. "Last chance to make that wish…"

"Go," she said on a laugh as she snatched the hat from his hand and watched him stride toward the bathroom. She wasn't one for making wishes, but if she were…

Could Clay Forrester really be as perfect as he seemed? She set the hat aside to straighten the pillows on the couch and pick up her shoes. Eleanor had complimented her for finding the perfect man to play Santa, but she'd had little to do with it.

Hearing the bathroom door open, Holly realized he'd finished changing before she'd finished her musing or looked for something to wear. She turned to face him, and the shoes she'd picked up fell from her hands.

Adjusting the cuff on his tuxedo, he glanced up at her. "Is everything all right?"

Holly stared, barely managing a nod. The black tux fit him perfectly, emphasizing his broad shoulders and long legs. The same lock of hair she'd tucked under his Santa hat earlier fell across his forehead. Blue eyes watched her from beneath straight black brows. Chiseled bone structure emphasized a straight nose, prominent cheekbones and a strong jaw.

If a Hollywood movie star had stepped out of the TV and into her living room, Holly couldn't have been more impressed—or dismayed.

"Holly, is something wrong?" He took a step toward her, and she waved aside his concern.

"No, no, everything's fine. Except—" she gestured to his tuxedo "—you look ready for the inaugural ball!"

"Well, the party is at the Lakeshore Plaza."

His words called to mind the elegant hotel, which boasted celebrity visits, views of Lake Michigan and penthouse suites rumored to cost ten thousand dollars a night. Holly had never dared to set foot inside the imported marble foyer, fearing management would throw her out for breaking some "no shirt, no shoes, no six-figure income, no admittance" rule.

"I can't go to the Lakeshore Plaza. I have nothing to wear!" Not only would she make a fool of herself, but she'd embarrass Clay as well. Her wardrobe would be a dead giveaway that she didn't belong.

He rolled his eyes. "I have never met a woman who thought she had enough clothes. Come on."

"Where are we going?" she asked when he grabbed her hand.

"Your bedroom."

"What!"

He tossed her a grin over his shoulder. "To find you something to wear."

"I work in a flower shop!" Holly protested as he pulled her through the doorway. The intimacy of Clay invading her bedroom sent heat rushing to her cheeks. She determinedly adverted her gaze from the tousled bed a mere three feet away. "I don't have nice clothes."

He turned to face her. His appraising look swept her from head to toe. "I like that."

Holly glanced down to see if her clothes had been magically transformed. "A sweater and jeans?" she asked, arching her eyebrows in disbelief.

"Hanging on a rack, that's a sweater and jeans. On you, it's something else entirely."

A delicious shiver raced through her at his husky words and the sexual appreciation darkening his eyes. She longed to give in to the attraction, but her survival instinct raged against it. "I can't wear this to the Lakeshore Plaza."

Undaunted, he pulled open her closet door. "So we'll find something else."

Holly watched him sort through the garments, his masculine hands a sensual contrast against the feminine fabrics. When he ran a hand down an empty sleeve, she swore she felt the intimate caress along her arm.

Eventually he pulled out a black satin and lace garment. "What about this?"

Holly fought an irrational blush. "*That* is a slip."

"Really?" He took a closer look. "With dress styles these days, it's hard to tell." His eyes glowed as he held the slip up to her body, and she felt as exposed as if he'd caught her wearing nothing more than the intimate lingerie. "Although that does explain why I like it."

"Great." She took the slip and shoved it back in the closet. "If I let you pick the outfit, I'll end up going to the party in my underwear."

Almost desperately, she flipped through her clothes. She had to find something before her entire wardrobe was touched with Clay's memory. Finally, a long black skirt caught her attention.

Holly held it up for him to see. "How about this?"

"That's good for a start. Now, all we need is this," Clay said as he brought the slip out again.

She shook her head. "Clay, I told you—"

Ignoring her, he pulled a black cropped jacket from the closet. "And this."

Holly started to protest until she took a look at the separate items he'd selected. With its spaghetti straps and lace trim, the top of the slip could pass for a camisole. Fashioned from similar materials, the skirt and jacket looked like a matched outfit.

Handing the hangers to her, he said, "Get dressed, and we can arrive at the party fashionably late."

The moment he left the room, Holly kicked off her shoes. If not for her, Clay would already be at the party. She dressed quickly and swept her hair into a twist before adding a hint of color to her lips and cheeks.

Taking a deep breath, Holly stepped back and scrutinized her image. She searched for any telltale sign that would reveal she didn't belong at a high-class party and found it in the insecurity swirling in her eyes.

"I'll be right out."

Clay heard Holly's voice drift through the bedroom's closed door. By the time they arrived, the party would be in full swing, and he'd seriously owe Marie for covering for him.

Walking around, he studied the living room, trying to glean some information about the intriguing woman who lived there. Nothing. No hint of friends, family, no insight into Holly's personal life. Even more curious was the lack of a Christmas tree. The woman who had staged such a wonderful evening for the foster children hadn't decorated her own home.

In the kitchen, Clay found a few personal details. A windowsill above the sink housed a variety of thriving plants, and crayon drawings and finger paintings plastered the refrigerator.

"Those are from the kids at Hopewell House."

He turned. Holly stood in the kitchen doorway, and he forgot all about the artwork. He'd known the long, straight skirt and simple jacket would compliment Holly's slender figure, but he hadn't expected the jeans and sweater she'd worn earlier to conceal such alluring curves. His eyes followed the slit in her skirt as it inched up her long legs. The skirt clung to her hips, and his hands itched to outline the shapely silhouette. Silk hugged her breasts beneath the jacket, and the edging of lace hinted at enticing cleavage.

Holly had piled her chestnut hair atop her head, leaving a few tendrils to curl around her face. The elegant style emphasized her cheekbones and almond-shaped eyes.

"The older kids drew the giraffe and the clown," she was saying.

Clay tore his gaze away to refocus on the artwork. He'd mistaken the giraffe and clown for a dog and a flower. "And what about…" He didn't have the slightest idea what the splotchy paintings were supposed to be. "The rest?"

"Lucas did the finger painting. The Hopewell sisters won't let him use crayons." When Clay raised a questioning eyebrow, Holly explained, "He eats them."

She reached over and straightened one of the pictures. Tenderness filled her gaze. Clearly, volunteering at the foster home wasn't something Holly reserved for the holidays. She cherished the drawings they gave her, yet she had no mementos of her own.

"We should probably get going," Holly said as she walked toward the living room. "I've made you late enough as it is."

"You were worth the wait."

Holly glanced over her shoulder as he helped with her coat, but the lift of her eyebrow revealed more doubt than pleasure.

In the back of the limo, Clay couldn't help studying Holly's elegant profile in the flickering shadow and light as they drove through the city streets. In those stop-action flashes, the slope of her forehead, the tilt of her nose and the curve of her lips could have been carved from marble, but there was nothing hard or cold about Holly.

She had a warmth and softness about her, but Clay sensed that circle of welcome didn't extend to everyone. Right now, she'd allowed him inside because of the night Santa had given to the kids she loved. But it would take more than that if he wanted to stay within that sphere.

If he wanted to…

He shouldn't even think about starting a relationship. Not

now. Not when he had his family business to right and his father's legacy of decimating struggling companies to rewrite.

But it's only one night, argued a voice that sounded suspiciously like his assistant's, Marie's. And he wasn't quite ready to step outside Holly's circle.

Heat blew from the vents, tantalizing Clay with the flower fresh scent of her perfume, and he reached out to brush a tendril of hair back from the curve of her cheek. "You look amazing."

She offered him a quick smile as she shifted toward him on the seat, the curl slipping from his grasp. "I know what you're doing."

Clay knew what he was doing, too, though not as deftly as usual if Holly was ready to call him on his seduction. "What's that?"

"You're trying to convince me I'm not going to stick out like a sore thumb."

Even in the shifting light, he read the sincerity in her expression. She really didn't know how beautiful she was.

"Holly." He started to deny her words until he saw that stubborn tilt to her chin. Changing tactics, he agreed, "You *are* going to stick out, but there's nothing we can do." Her eyes widened as he leaned forward. "Beautiful women have a way of attracting attention."

Disbelief lingered in her gaze, and Clay tempted himself with the thought of proving his words with a kiss. Pulse pounding, he lifted a hand toward her face. The bright glare of the dome light caught him off guard, and he looked over his shoulder in frustration. Behind his waiting driver was the well-lit Lakeshore Plaza Hotel.

Clay hadn't even noticed the car stopping. If the ride had lasted a few minutes longer…make that a few *hours* longer… Shaking off the tempting thoughts, he climbed from the limo and held out his hand to Holly. Her fingers felt cold and fragile in his palm. With a reassuring squeeze, he told her, "Remember, it's just a party."

Together they stepped through the front doors, and Holly's breath caught. She'd heard glowing descriptions of the hotel and even seen a picture or two, but her imagination hadn't captured the opulence.

Floor-to-ceiling paintings decorated the lobby, and a waterfall cascaded down the wall behind the front desk. Holly had to force herself not to tip her head back and stare at the gold and crystal chandelier. But as incredible as the decor was, nothing compared to her amazement at walking into the Lakeshore Plaza with Clay Forrester.

A uniformed bellhop gave them directions to the ballroom. He tipped his cap to Holly. "Enjoy your evening."

As Clay led her to the ballroom, music and laughter filled the air, the happy noise punctuated by a cork popping. Several people called out greetings, and Clay grabbed two flutes of champagne from a passing waiter. Handing one to Holly, he raised his own in a toast. "To you, Holly, for reminding me of the meaning of Christmas."

His words sent a giddy rush pouring through her, and Holly didn't need champagne's intoxicating promise, but she took a small sip, anyway. Then another, enjoying the way the bubbles danced on her tongue. Smiling at her obvious pleasure, Clay said, "Like it?"

"It's amazing. I've never had champagne before."

Holly didn't need to see his eyebrows lift to realize her mistake. *Champagne and caviar,* Holly reminded herself, embarrassed to have pointed out her own naïveté.

"The first time I had champagne was at my cousin's wedding. I think I was seventeen." With anyone else, Holly might have suspected Clay's story was meant to reveal his own sophistication, but the way he held her gaze reassured her his story held a different meaning. After taking a drink of his own champagne, he said, "I'll never forget that night or that first taste."

, Holly didn't need champagne to make the night memorable. Clay had already done that. And as much as she enjoyed the drink, his lips pressed to hers would be a far more unforgettable first taste.

Her gaze lowered to his mouth at the thought, and Clay's eyes darkened. "Holly—"

"Well, it's about time you showed up," a feminine voice called out. Holly looked over her shoulder to see a stunning brunette with close-cropped hair sashay toward them. She wore a red sequined dress that would have done a 1920s flapper proud. "When you said 'a little late,' I thought you meant fifteen minutes. I've had a heck of a time covering for you."

Looking around at the party in full swing, Clay said wryly, "I can see I've been missed."

"Okay, so we started without you, but I'm glad you're here." Lowering her voice, she added, "Albert Jensen's started working the room like tonight was his idea."

Holly saw Clay's jaw tighten at the words, but then he caught her gaze, and the tension drained away. Relaxing into a smile, he said, "Sounds like we're just in time. How's everything else going?"

"Great. Except for the Santa. Where did you find that guy?"

Holly and Clay exchanged a glance. "Why? What's wrong?"

"Nothing. Except he drinks like a fish and hasn't moved from the buffet table."

Holly looked over. Sure enough, Charlie in his Santa suit held a plate piled high with food. His beard was pulled down below his chin as he ate half a piece of cheesecake in one bite.

"I'd say he's perfect for this group," Clay joked.

Marie shook her head and held out her hand to Holly. "I'm Marie Cirillo, Clay's assistant."

"Holly Bainbridge."

Marie cocked her head. "You look familiar."

Holly shot a worried glance in Clay's direction, unsure how to respond. How would he explain bringing a shop clerk to this elegant party? But Clay didn't bother with explanations. He simply said, "Holly works at the flower shop in our building."

"Of course." Marie's smile remained; so did the touch of curiosity. "I bought a plant there."

"An ivy, wasn't it? They're one of my favorites," said Holly.

Marie winced. "Mine, too. But the leaves started to turn yellow, and now they're kinda brown."

Clay laughed. "Marie kills plants since the Humane Society won't allow her to have pets."

Marie stuck her tongue out at her boss, and Holly laughed. "You could be overwatering," she said, "and you might try some iron."

"Thanks. I'll do that," Marie said. Then, turning to Clay, she demanded, "Why do I put up with you?"

"Because we're perfect for each other. No one else will work for me, and no one else will employ you."

"Is that it?" Marie grabbed a glass from a passing waiter and winked. "I thought it was for the free champagne and cheesecake."

Nodding at the glass, he toasted, "Then consider yourself well compensated for the evening, and keep Holly company while I go talk to the DJ." With a quick squeeze to Holly's arm, he promised, "I'll be right back."

Holly opened her mouth to ask him to stay or offer to go with him, then closed it before she could reveal how nervous she was. Without Clay at her side, her insecurities came rushing back, and she glanced around, waiting for everyone to notice she didn't belong. She didn't have to wait long.

"You know, I saw Clay right before the party. He didn't mention bringing a date."

Holly swallowed. "It was pretty last minute."

"I guess so." Marie's expression softened slightly at Holly's obvious discomfort, and she said, "Sorry. You must think I'm horribly nosy. It's just that you're the first woman Clay's bothered introducing to me since his divorce."

"Clay was married?"

Marie winced. "Me and my big mouth."

"No, it's okay." There was no reason for Clay to tell her about his ex-wife. This wasn't a real date or the beginning of a relationship. Which was a good thing. If it *had* been real, Holly would have worried about the image in her mind of the woman Clay had married. Someone sophisticated, stylish, with a pedigree to match his own. A woman who would never need help dressing for a party…

But there was no reason to worry, because it wasn't real, Holly insisted as Clay walked back over, ignoring the flash of attraction that felt 100 percent genuine.

"Sorry about that," Clay said. "Duty calls. I hope Marie hasn't been spilling all my secrets."

"Just one," Marie confessed, with a guilty glance at Holly. A champagne cork popped nearby, and she added, "That bottle is calling my name. See you!"

As Marie made her escape, Clay looked at Holly. Seeming unconcerned by the secrets his assistant might have revealed, he said, "As incredible as it seems, I don't know what I'd do without her. She keeps me sane. This past year, that was a full-time job."

It was the second time Clay had mentioned business troubles. He had such a commanding presence, Holly had a hard time imagining a problem Clay couldn't solve by force of will alone. A company didn't gain wealth and reputation like Forrester Industries without a man at the top who could forge through difficulties with the subtlety of a battering ram.

An image of Clay dressed as Santa rose in her mind. Who was he really? A man who cared enough about a group of foster children to give them a Christmas they'd always remember? Or the businessman with a ruthless reputation?

"If it isn't our fearless leader."

Tensing at the greeting, Clay turned and nodded at the silver-haired man who strutted toward them, champagne glass in hand. "Evening, Jensen."

"This is some party," the man said, his narrowed gaze sweeping the elegant ballroom.

"The employees deserve it. It's been a challenging year."

Jensen snorted. "*Challenging* is right, with all the changes you've made. But what the hell?" he added, waving his hand at the surrounding ballroom. "Nothing like buying company loyalty, right?"

He laughed, but the tension crackling between the two men told Holly that Jensen wasn't joking. No humor existed in the man's beady eyes, which gleamed with thinly disguised malice.

"I'm not trying to buy anything or *anyone*. The employees are loyal because they understand the changes I'm making are for the best."

"The best for whom? Not for the company, that's for damn sure. Your father understood—"

"My father understood a great many things when it came to business," Clay interrupted. His words cutting off abruptly, he took a deep breath, his shoulders rolling beneath the crisp tuxedo jacket as he visibly forced himself to relax. "But when it comes people, I know a thing or two my father didn't."

Jensen's ruddy complexion darkened, but Clay never gave the man the opportunity to argue. The band switched to a slow song, and he grabbed Holly's hand. "If you'll excuse us, I owe my date a dance."

Holly had no choice but to follow Clay to the dance floor. The glittering chandelier spun overhead as he twirled her around, leaving her light-headed and breathless. Not just from his dizzying, sure-footed steps, but from intimate contact. With a wobbly laugh, she said, "Being around you certainly keeps a woman on her toes."

As if the confrontation with Jensen had never taken place, Clay flashed a smile. "Don't worry. I promise not to step on them."

"That's not what I mean," she chided. "First, you maneuvered me into coming to this party, and now onto the dance floor."

"Hey, I didn't *maneuver* you. I asked. You said yes." Confidence shone in his blue eyes, as if her answer had never been in doubt.

And, really, what other answer could she have given? The whole night had been filled with magic. Santa had come to Hopewell House, thanks to Clay, but once again Holly warned herself not to let emotion carry her away. She'd seen it before at Hopewell House and throughout her childhood in foster homes, especially around the holidays.

People were filled with good cheer and high spirits. Donations of toys, food, and money rolled in, but by New Year's, the good cheer, the high spirits, and the needy children were forgotten.

No matter how wonderful Clay might seem, he, too, would disappear. Best to simply enjoy the moment and not to look ahead. And right now, wrapped in his arms, she found the moment so easy to enjoy.

"You *did* say yes," Clay reminded her when she remained silent for so long.

Striving for a light tone, she replied, "Of course, I said yes. What was it Marie said? Something about an inability to resist free champagne and cheesecake?"

He gave a mock groan. "I can see I'll have to keep the two of you apart in the future."

Clay spun her into an elegant turn, and she caught sight of Jensen on the sidelines. A frown still twisted his face, and he looked to be in a heated discussion with two other men.

She wondered about the changes Clay had referred to and the loyalty Jensen thought he was trying to buy. Did some employees disapprove of the company's "take-no-prisoners" attitude? *Was* the party an attempt to bribe his own people?

Only hours before, Holly might have thought so, but now denial rose inside her. She'd seen the respect his employees showed. Respect money couldn't buy. And even though she couldn't forget the heartbreak and humiliation written on the old man's face when he accused Clay of destroying his family's company, she no longer knew what to believe.

Clay spun her once more beneath the chandelier, and her breath caught as his muscular thighs brushed against hers. The unspoken awareness in his eyes left her feeling weak. Her knees nearly buckled, and her hand tightened on his shoulder.

She knew what she *wanted* to believe, but she'd put her faith in people before only to be let down. Mark was the latest in a list of disappointments that went back as far as she could remember.

Unbidden, a memory came to mind of the Parkers, smiling at her. "We've got a big house and a nice yard where our dog loves to play. There are plenty of kids in our neighborhood you can make friends with. We can't wait for you to come live with us."

She'd been five at the time, young enough to still care about things like yards and dogs and kids to play with, but most of all she'd wanted a family, and the Parkers were supposed to be hers. Everyone had promised. The Parkers, her caseworker, her foster family at the time. And she'd believed them, but in the end, the most important lesson learned was that promises, not rules, were made to be broken.

As the music faded away, Holly stepped out of Clay's arms and pulled her hand from his to applaud the musicians. It was an excuse to reclaim some much-needed distance. His knowing gaze called her on her cowardice, but saving face wasn't nearly as important as protecting her heart.

Guiding her off the dance floor, Clay stopped at the dessert table. "Here, you have to try this." He loaded a plate for the two of them, cut off a piece of cheesecake, and held out the fork. "Marie went to great lengths to save these from certain frost-bite."

Holly leaned forward to take a bite. Strawberries topped the dessert, the sweet taste combining with the rich, creamy, melt-in-your-mouth filling. Pulling back, she found Clay watching closely. Her tongue streaked out to catch a stray crumb, and his eyes darkened with undisguised desire. Her skin tingled from that heated look, anticipating his touch. When he brushed his thumb against the corner of her mouth, she almost groaned in longing.

His voice hoarse, he asked, "How was it?"

"It—it was delicious."

Clay cupped her jaw, but the intensity in his gaze held her motionless. Alarm bells rang, the warning drowned out by her pounding heartbeat, as he bent his head and kissed her. The ballroom faded away until she was aware only of his fingers curving over her jaw and his mouth, warm and persuasive, against her own. Better than cheesecake, better than champagne, better than anything she could imagine. She wanted nothing more than for the kiss to go on and on....

Instead, as Clay drew back, she reluctantly opened her eyes, focusing on his handsome face, backlit by the winking chandelier.

"I have to agree," he murmured. "Delicious."

Chapter Four

Clay leaned back against the limo's leather seat. Satisfaction gave a greater buzz than champagne as he recalled the employees' laughter and cheers as he called the winning numbers, raffling off electronics, Chicago Bulls basketball tickets and gift certificates to some of the finest local restaurants.

The party had been an unquestionable success. This date, however, was another matter, he thought, with a sideways glance at Holly. She'd fallen silent during the ride back to her apartment. Memories of their kiss tantalized him. He'd taken her off guard, but surprise hadn't dimmed her sweet response. The thought alone quickened his heart rate, and the success of the evening gave him confidence that his luck would continue.

"The party was wonderful," Holly complimented, her polite tone creating an unwanted distance.

Still, he felt a touch of pride as he said, "Not bad for a first time."

"You've never had a company party before?"

Clay shook his head. "No. My father believed in keeping personal and professional lives separate."

"But you think the two can coexist?"

"Actually, I've been accused of focusing too much on business. Tonight made me want to pay more attention to my personal life."

"Clay." He heard the hesitation in her voice as she shifted to face him. "I really want to thank you. What you did for the kids—"

Interrupting, he said, "Holly, I was glad to do it. But that's not what tonight was about. At least, not for me."

He waited for her to say the same, to admit that she'd gone with him for a reason other than gratitude, but she stayed silent. His confidence slipping, he tried again. "I asked you out because you're a beautiful, desirable woman."

This time, Holly's breath caught, and she turned her face toward the window. She was *so* close, close enough for the scent of her perfume to tease his senses, close enough that if he reached out, he could trail his fingers along her leg, exposed by the tantalizing slit of her skirt. But even with only a few inches separating them, she maintained a distance he didn't know how to breach.

"The holidays are a magical time, aren't they?" she asked softly, her attention on the store windows, with their draping garland, red and gold bows, and flashing, colorful lights. "All the decorating, the shopping for the right gift, the planning for the perfect meal. It's so wonderful at the time, but then it's over, and you can't help but feel disappointed."

Reading between the lines, Clay heard what Holly didn't say. This one night was all they would have. The rejection took him off guard, even more so than the desire pulsing hot and fast in his veins.

But he'd caught a glimpse of Holly's life, the love and self-lessness she showed the kids at Hopewell House. She wasn't the type to go for a lighthearted fling. And with his attention focused on business, he didn't have time for more.

Even if he did, marriage had taught him he lacked whatever it took to keep a woman happy in the long run. Why face that failure, that inadequacy inside himself again? Letting Holly go now would be best for both of them.

So why couldn't he do it?

"I know what you mean. The disappointment when a moment that starts out so bright and beautiful comes to an end. But there's one thing you forgot."

Swallowing, Holly turned back and whispered, "What's that?"

"The holidays are just getting started."

In the shifting glow of passing streetlights, he saw her eyes widen and her gaze drop to his lips. "Clay."

His name was less of a protest than a plea, and instant arousal answered. The loose curls of her upswept hair teased his knuckles as he cupped her nape and pulled her close. Her lips were already parted for him, and desire exploded at the first touch. He sank into the rich leather seat, bringing Holly with him. He slanted his mouth over hers, teasing, tasting, advancing, retreating…and she was right there with him, silently urging him on, her hands clutching his shoulders, her tongue drawing him deeper.

With Holly's breasts teasing his chest, it was all Clay could do to keep his free hand at her waist. He wanted to feel her flesh in his hands, her skin against his. Wanted to hear her soft sounds of pleasure as her body welcomed his.

In the dim recess of his mind, he realized the limo's subtle motion had ceased. He wished he could somehow signal his driver to keep going. Somewhere, anywhere, so long as it meant he and Holly never had to open the doors to reality.

But even as he reluctantly lifted his mouth from hers, it was obvious in her wide-eyed regret that reality had already sunk in. Immediately pulling away from him, she stammered, "That shouldn't have...*we* shouldn't have—"

The overhead light flared as the door opened, and Clay squinted at the sudden glare. Without waiting, Holly scrambled from the car, barely accepting the driver's help. Clay caught up with her in two long strides and took her arm. "I'm walking you to your door," he said in a voice that didn't allow for protest.

Silently, they entered the building and climbed the flights of stairs. At her apartment, she turned to face him, her back to the door. He knew better than to expect an invitation inside, but he wasn't giving up now. Not after that kiss.

He'd never expected it to go so far. How could he? A kiss had never *taken* him so far.

"I want to see you again, Holly."

"Clay, we have nothing in common," she protested. "Nothing—"

"Nothing but an explosive sexual attraction."

Holly's lashes fell, but not in time to hide the acknowledgement in her gaze. Still, she shook her head. "I can't. I'm sorry."

Holly slipped inside the apartment, with a whispered "Merry Christmas." She eased the door shut, leaving Clay out in the cold. He was starting to walk away when he remembered the Santa suit he'd left in her apartment.

With a glance back at Holly's doorway, he smiled and jogged down the stairs. At the very least, he had an excuse to see her again.

"Here comes Santa Claus..."

As Clay walked by his assistant's desk, he heard Marie singing beneath her breath and glared a warning she was bound to ignore.

She'd been like a dog gnawing a bone ever since he'd arrived at work Monday morning to find his garment bag already hanging in his office. Holly had given the Santa suit to Marie, leaving him to explain how he'd left it at Holly's apartment.

So much for seeing Holly again, Clay thought. That should have been the end of it. Unfortunately, he hadn't been able to keep her off his mind. Too often, he found her sneaking into his thoughts when he should have been concentrating on business.

"Oh, come on!" Marie followed him into his office. She pulled the paint cloth off one of the chairs and sat down. "Why won't you tell me about you and Holly?"

"There is *no* me and Holly. She turned me down." When his assistant studied him silently, he demanded, "What?"

"I guess I'm not that surprised."

"Gee, thanks. Remind me never to come to you for compliments."

Marie laughed. "I just meant that I don't think you're the type of guy that Holly dates."

Clay wasn't sure he liked the idea of Holly dating other guys. She'd turned him down, and he preferred to think that meant she wasn't dating anyone. "What type of guy is that?"

"Most guys take a girl to the movies on a first date. You took Holly to a black-tie dinner with a hundred people she didn't know."

"I didn't mean to make her uncomfortable." But he *had* pushed her into going, thinking he could ease her out of her self-consciousness. Evidently, he'd failed.

"All I'm saying is that you live life in the fast lane, and Holly's probably worried that she can't keep up." Marie stood. "No one likes being left behind."

She left the office, and the door clicked shut. He hadn't been kidding when he told Holly his assistant kept him sane. He could always count on Marie to keep him in line. No doubt he didn't thank her enough.

Clay smiled. He knew the perfect way to show his appreciation.

* * *

The bell above the door rang, and Holly called out, "I'll be right with you." She slid the last floral arrangement into the refrigerator and turned, a polite smile on her face. "How can I…"

Clay Forrester stood in the doorway. Plants and flowers crowded almost every inch of the shop, and he ducked beneath a philodendron as he stepped inside.

After the magical night, Holly had been convinced her mind had played tricks on her. His eyes couldn't have been so blue; his shoulders so wide; his smile so devastating. With a growing sense of dismay, she realized she'd been right. But the trick was on her, because her memory had failed to live up to reality. Every little detail was so much more vivid and breathtaking than she recalled.

"Clay, hi."

"Hi." He looked around the shop with curiosity. "I need to send some flowers."

Flowers? Her face burned with embarrassment. "Oh, I see." Straightening her shoulders, she put her most professional foot forward. She stepped from behind the counter and said, "I have some examples you can look at."

Holly opened a book on the counter. She'd planned to back away while he looked at the floral-arrangement photographs, but he stepped behind her. Gazing over her shoulder, he trapped her between the counter and his own body. The scent of his cologne mingled with the gardenias near the counter, masculine and feminine combining. Holly gripped the counter, feeling her knees go weak.

Stop it! He's here buying flowers for another woman!

"How's that?" Her voice cracked as she pointed blindly to an exotic arrangement of orchids.

"Not bad," he murmured.

Like a tuning fork, her entire body hummed with the vibrations of his voice. "So, is that it?" she asked almost desperately.

"Not quite. I'll know what I want when I see it."

"What?" She made the mistake of turning toward him. Their faces were mere inches apart. Against her will, her gaze dropped to his mouth. Sculpted to perfection, his lips looked firm, yet she remembered the seductive feel of them against her own. Her heartbeat quickened, and an excited trembling overtook her.

"The flowers," he reminded her. "I'll know what I want when I see it."

Holly forced herself to take a deep breath, even though it meant inhaling his enticing scent, and turned the page. She'd started to fear the book would never end when Clay wrapped an arm around her waist and pointed to a picture. "What about that one?"

"Um…" She blinked, trying to focus.

He'd picked an assortment of daisies and irises, mixed with a few red carnations. Arranged in a brown wicker basket and topped with a yellow bow, the flowers were bright and friendly. "Very nice."

"I'll take them."

Holly breathed a sigh of relief when Clay backed away. She pulled out a card and envelope for him to sign. Still standing at his side, she was tempted to look and see what he wrote. But it was none of her business whom he sent flowers to. They'd had one date, and she'd turned him down for a second, Holly reminded herself, suffering a moment's regret and ignoring the underlying jealousy.

"Where would you like the flowers delivered?"

"To my office. They're for Marie."

"Oh. For Marie." Green-eyed monsters suddenly transformed into happy butterflies in her stomach. "I wanted to thank you for the candy you sent," she said once she rang up his order.

Clay chuckled. "Sending flowers seemed somewhat redundant."

"Chocolate was a good choice."

After turning Clay down for a second date, Holly hadn't expected to hear from him again, let alone receive a box of gourmet chocolates the very next day. The flavor of chocolate-covered strawberries had burst on her tongue with all the pleasure of a spring day. But it was the memory the strawberries evoked, memories of Clay's kiss beneath the sparkling chandelier, that had her savoring one after another until she'd eaten nearly the whole box.

Clay glanced at his watch and said, "It's almost twelve. Would you like to get something to eat?"

"I'm not sure that's a good idea."

He shrugged. "Hey, it's not my idea. Eating lunch at noon has been a common practice for years." When his teasing didn't convince her, he said, "Just lunch at the sandwich shop a few blocks away, I swear. No champagne toasts involved."

His words took her by surprise, though she should have known he'd sensed her discomfort. Clay really seemed too good to be true and far too easy to fall for. And then where would she be? Holly didn't know how she'd captured Clay's attention, but she knew she couldn't hold on to it for long. He'd move on to someone better—someone prettier, someone smarter, someone with a background equal to his own.

But when she opened her mouth to explain all that, the words didn't come. "I can't go until Marilyn is done with her break," she surprised herself by saying. "Why don't I come up to your office once she gets back?"

"All right. See you then." He gave a brief wave before he ducked beneath the hanging philodendron and left the shop.

"See you," Holly echoed softly, a faint buzz of warning following quickly on the heels of anticipation.

When she stepped out of the elevator a half hour later, nerves somersaulted in her stomach. It was just lunch! But she feared it could be so much more. The beginning of something she didn't know if she wanted to start.

"Hello, Holly." Marie pointed to the double doors beyond her desk. "Clay's expecting you. Go on in."

"Thanks." Even with Marie's permission, Holly knocked first before opening the door and taking her first look around the office.

Scaffolding stretched across one wall. A tarp crackled beneath her feet. Tape covered the window, and a half-built bookshelf ran the length of one wall. Clay sat in a high-backed black leather chair behind a monstrosity of a desk—both clearly leftovers from the office's previous decor.

"Wow. You weren't kidding about the remodeling."

Clay shook his head, exasperation ringing in his voice as he said, "It's been like this for weeks. Ready to go? I'm starving."

"Me, too."

Clay stopped at the reception area long enough to ask his assistant, "Did you want me to bring you anything back for lunch?"

"No, thanks," Marie answered. "I'll grab something later. Have a good time."

Holly couldn't be sure, but she thought she saw Marie give Clay a subtle wink. Out in the hall, he pressed the elevator button. As Holly caught his gaze, she asked, "Think the elevator's safe?"

"No one's working in my office, so it should be okay." Despite his words, when the bell above the elevator rang, they both hesitated.

Clay laughed and took her arm, and together they crossed the threshold. The doors shut, and a faint hum accompanied the gradual descent. As unlikely as it seemed, Holly half expected the elevator to shudder to a halt, but the bell rang, and the doors slid open.

"Safe and sound," he said.

Just the way she wanted it, Holly insisted, ignoring the slight twinge of disappointment.

Seated at a corner table, Holly and Clay found enough privacy in the crowded deli to have a quiet conversation. They'd ordered sandwiches at the counter, turkey and sprouts with light mayo for her, pastrami with hot mustard for Clay. During lunch, they kept the conversation light, focusing on favorite foods, music, and movies, surprising Holly with how much they had in common.

At his company party, in a ballroom lit by crystal chandeliers and flowing with champagne toasts, she'd vividly recalled the differences in their lives. But seated in the cracked vinyl booth, surrounded by the scent of frying hamburgers and the sound of the cook gruffly calling out orders to the waitresses, it was harder to remember.

Of course, she thought wryly, his tailored suit and boldly patterned silk tie served as obvious indications, but Holly was starting to see beyond the handsome, sophisticated veneer to the real man beneath.

Only after they finished eating did the conversation turn more serious as Clay again mentioned the seemingly unending work on his office. She stirred her hot tea, buying some time. She sensed something else fueled his aggravation. "At the party, you mentioned making some changes, but I have the feeling you weren't talking about redecorating," she said tentatively as she also recalled Jensen's insinuations that Clay's father wouldn't approve.

In all the years she'd spent imagining what it would be like to have a family, she'd never considered the demands that came with having relatives. Had Clay wanted to run the family business, or had the responsibility fallen on him when his father died? Either way, the pressure must have been enormous.

"No," Clay said on a sigh as he leaned back against the booth. "It's not about redecorating my office. It's about reversing the company's philosophy of profiting off other people's misery. I don't want to make a living by taking a bad situation and making it worse. I want to go in, fix the problem, and make things better for everyone."

Holly's eyes widened. She didn't know what surprised her more—Clay's view of his own company or his plan to completely change its direction. But he must have taken her silence as something other than surprise.

Smiling, he said, "Sorry. Bad habit. But I've learned my lesson. No boring business talk."

"No, it's not that," Holly protested even as she wondered who had taught him that lesson. The ex-wife Marie had mentioned at the party? "I'm not bored. I'm...amazed."

"I'm not sure there's anything *amazing* about it."

"I don't know what else you could call it." And if Holly hadn't already thought *Clay* was amazing, this latest revelation would have definitely convinced her. "Although I shouldn't be surprised. Not after the way you stepped in and solved the problem of the missing Santa for the Hopewell children."

"A Santa that wouldn't have been missing in the first place if not for me," he pointed out.

"Yes, but you didn't know—"

"Because I didn't bother to ask. I pretty much did the same thing with the way my father ran the business. It all seemed so black and white. Or maybe I should say red and black. If a company was in trouble, Forrester Industries would buy the business, bring in our own people to save it if we could, sell it off if we couldn't."

"But it's not that simple, is it?"

"No, it's not that simple. And I'm not so sure my father's way of doing business was even that ethical." Clay frowned out the window, his gaze locked on the past. "A man came into the building a few weeks after my father died, and some of the things he said…"

"I was there that day," Holly interjected. When Clay's gaze swung back to her, she quickly explained, "I wasn't eavesdropping. I was locking up the shop and couldn't help overhearing."

Leaning forward until the barrier of the table between them seemed to disappear, Clay said, "I wanted to argue. I wanted to tell that man my father wouldn't have lied, he wouldn't have made promises unless he fully intended to follow through, and if he failed to save the business, it was only because the business couldn't be saved. That's what I *wanted* to say, what I wanted to believe."

His frustration called out to her, and she wanted to help, the way he'd helped her by playing Santa for the kids. One friend reaching out to another. Reaching out to smooth the frown from his forehead, to tease the tension from his jaw, to outline the sexy, seductive line of his lips…

Holly jerked her hands into her lap, just in case they decided to get a little *too* friendly.

"But you don't believe it."

"The truth is my father would do or say anything to get what he wanted. If he turned the company around, great. But he'd turn his back on a promise in a heartbeat if it meant Forrester Industries would make a buck."

"And you're going to change all that."

Clay laughed. "I wish everyone had your confidence."

Holly felt her face heat. She hadn't meant to come off like a one-woman cheer squad, but with Clay's determination, it was easy to believe he would succeed. "I think you can accomplish anything you put your mind to. But it might take some time. It isn't easy to let go of the past."

"That's been the hardest part. As a kid, I thought my parents knew everything. They never made mistakes or screwed up. Now, as an adult, I've come to realize my father was far from perfect. But it's hard to see him knocked from this childhood pedestal. You know?"

Holly looked into Clay's eyes, into a startling blue gaze that expected understanding, and panicked. The earlier connection broke as if the wiring had somehow snapped. Such a small thing, but the words reminded her that she wasn't like other people. She didn't know anything about exalting parents, about placing them on glorious pedestals.

She knew nothing about normal families at all.

Grabbing her purse, she reached inside, pulled out a ten-dollar bill, and tossed it on the table. "I've got to get back to work."

Clay sat back in surprise as she slid from the booth. "What? Holly, wait! Let me walk with you."

"That's okay." She swirled her coat around her shoulders. "I'll be fine."

She raced past crowded booths and out the swinging glass door, into the swirling snow, before he had the chance to call for the check. Clutching her coat tightly, she turned into the frigid wind, blinking her stinging eyes.

She never should have gone to lunch with Clay. The differences in their lives went far beyond wealth or social status. No matter what pressure he'd felt as the only son, he was a man with strong family connections, while she had no family, no connections at all.

You could have told him, her conscience chided.

But Mark was the last man she'd talked to about her childhood, and he'd taught a hard-won lesson about trusting other people with her past...or her future.

Chapter Five

"If going out with Holly means I get flowers, I'm going to schedule the two of you for a lunch date every day," Marie said as Clay walked in the office.

The bouquet took center stage on her desk, filling the space with color and an earthy, floral scent that reminded him of Holly. "It was lunch. Don't make too big of a deal out of it," he said, the warning as much for him as it was for Marie.

With the way Holly had rushed from the deli, he doubted another date was in their future. It was the second time she'd all but run from him. After marriage to Victoria, a woman who wanted him for his family name and social status, he'd fallen for a woman who didn't want him at all.

Fallen for?

No, no way. Clay shoved the thought aside. They'd had one and a half dates, if lunch counted, and a couple of amazing kisses. Hardly anything that amounted to a serious relationship.

So what was it about Holly's gentle spirit that had him

spilling his guts? He'd told her about his family, his father, things he never discussed with anyone. And Holly, well, she could be guarding state secrets for all the personal details she revealed.

"Enjoy the flowers, Marie," he told his assistant over his shoulder as he walked toward his office.

"Oh, Clay, wait! I forgot to tell you." He'd just pushed the door open when she called out, "Albert Jensen's waiting in your office."

Great, he thought, hiding his annoyance as he nodded at the older man. "Jensen." He rounded his desk and pointed at the tarp-covered chair. "Have a seat."

Jensen eyed the cluttered, under-construction office with displeasure. "I'll stand." Getting right to the point, he said, "Before you took over, your father had expressed an interest in JW Shipping."

Expressed an interest. That was one hell of a mild way to describe what his father had really meant. Forrester Industries expressing an interest in a company was similar to Attila the Hun setting his sights on a neighboring country.

Or at least it always had been.

"The company was in trouble, but they've pulled out of it."

Waving aside the argument, Jensen said, "John Westfell finagled a loan to pay off the worst of the company's debts. It's a quick fix at best, delaying the inevitable. Now's the time to make a move."

"I told you before, Albert, that isn't the way this company does business anymore."

The man's face flushed. "This company won't be doing any business if you keep letting sure things like this pass by!" Taking a deep breath, he started over with a more persuasive tone. "JW Shipping is going under. If we don't take the company, you better believe our competition will."

As much as Clay hated to admit it, Jensen was right. Not

doing anything might keep his conscience clean, but it wouldn't save the shipping company. Suddenly, the conversation with Holly at the deli came rushing back.

It isn't easy to let go of the past....

Hell, she was right. He hadn't let go. Jensen was conducting business as usual, and companies Clay refused to take over were simply swallowed whole by the competition. In the end, nothing had changed at all.

"You know what, Albert? You're right."

The man stopped in mid-tirade. Collecting himself, he stuck out his chest and gave a decisive nod. "It's about time you started seeing things clearly. Now, about JW Shipping—"

"Call John Westfell, and tell him we're interested in a limited partnership."

"A what?" Jensen's chest puffed out even farther, and Clay waited for him to blow.

"A partnership. Like you said, another company will take them over if we don't do something."

He'd made such offers before, investing in rather than taking over troubled companies, as he'd done with Hendrix Properties, but on a much smaller scale. Never a partnership, never such a large company, and never one Jensen had set his sights on.

"That is not what I meant! Your father didn't intend for this company to act as some kind of charity, rescuing businesses that fall on hard times."

Whatever disappointment his father might or might not have felt, fate had decreed Clay would never face it. What he did have to face, however, was himself in the mirror. And he couldn't do that if he ran the company the way his father had.

"I know," Clay admitted. "And I also know that's going to change. This isn't his company anymore, Albert, it's mine. Given time, there's more money to be made in saving a business like JW Shipping than there is in destroying it."

"*If* you save it," Jensen sneered. "And if you don't, you've tied yourself to a sinking company that will pull you down. Hell, that kind of failure is what you deserve, but I'll be damned if I watch it happen."

Looking at Jensen, his father's right-hand man, Clay made a decision. He could hold on to the past, or he could cut ties and look to the future. "Fine. I accept your resignation."

To Jensen's credit, he barely flinched. Shaking his head in disgust, he said, "I've said it all along. You're nothing like your father."

"And that," Clay said, "is the one thing we agree on."

Jensen stormed from the office, with a slam of the door. For Clay, it was like the door to the past closing. The tension twisting his shoulders into knots slid away, and an excitement took its place. Picking up the phone, he started making plans.

Half an hour later, he hung up, smiling in satisfaction. He had a project he could get behind, one that would help accomplish his goal to change the company's ruthless practices and reputation. It had taken a lot of convincing to get John Westfell to agree to meet with the company who'd threatened a hostile takeover, but Clay had insisted the meeting would be worthwhile.

Excitement churned inside him, and he felt like celebrating. No, he felt like celebrating with Holly. She was the only person he wanted to share this with, and even though he'd only seen her an hour ago, he wanted to rush downstairs to the flower shop despite his earlier decision to back off.

They'd gotten off to such a good start, but then she'd bolted. He replayed their conversation but couldn't think of anything he'd said to make her run. He did know one thing, though. He wasn't going to find out by second-guessing his every word.

I think you can accomplish anything you put your mind to, Holly had said.

Clay hoped she was right. Especially since he planned to focus that attention on her.

* * *

Eleanor Hopewell answered Clay's knock, her smile polite, but questioning. "May I help you?"

He'd gone to the flower shop to talk to Holly, but her coworker explained she'd taken the afternoon off for volunteer work. Clay had known exactly where to find her. "Is Holly Bainbridge here?"

The elderly woman frowned. "Can I ask who's looking for her?"

Fighting the temptation to say "Kris Kringle," he answered, "Clay Forrester."

"Mr. Forrester!" Eleanor's eyes lit behind her glasses. "I'm so sorry. I didn't recognize you! Please, come in!" She held the door open, and he stepped inside the warm house. "We really must thank you again for your help last week. It meant so much to the children, and Holly as well."

Clay slipped out of his jacket, and Eleanor hung it on one of the waist-high hooks behind the front door. "I enjoyed it," he told her, still somewhat surprised by that.

"Children do have a way of bringing out the kid in all of us. I wish more people would realize that volunteering is as much about receiving as it is about giving."

Thinking of the joy in Holly's eyes, Clay knew she would agree. "Holly spends a lot of time here, doesn't she?"

"Oh yes. My sister and I have run Hopewell House for years, but Holly has an understanding that surpasses our experience." Eleanor searched his expression. He wasn't sure what he was looking for, but she seemed satisfied with what she found. "She grew up in foster homes herself, you know."

He'd had no idea, but little wonder Holly had run out on him. He'd spent most of their lunch talking about his relationship with his father. She'd understood his complicated feelings so perfectly, he never guessed she'd grown up without family.

"I didn't realize…."

"Holly doesn't talk much about her childhood, but my sister and I, along with these children, are the closest thing to family she has."

A protective note entered Eleanor's voice. For the first time, Clay saw beyond the kindly softness in the woman's round face to the sharpness in her gaze. He half expected her to ask what his intentions were. Problem was, he didn't have an answer.

Hadn't he planned to back off? Wasn't Holly's longing for family reason enough to keep his distance? With Jensen's resignation, he had a greater incentive than ever to focus on business, yet his first instinct had been to see Holly, to talk to her about his plans.

"It's not right."

For a split second, Clay thought Eleanor had read his mind. Should he have stayed away? "What's not right?"

"For a girl like Holly to surround herself with old women and children. Not that we don't appreciate it," she added. "We do, but she needs the company of someone her own age."

Someone like you. Eleanor didn't say the words, but Clay heard them. His first impulse was to protest. Ever since the divorce, he'd resisted even the idea of emotional entanglements. But how could he argue when he was right there?

Fortunately, Eleanor didn't seem to expect a reply. To her, his mere presence was explanation enough. "Holly's in the kitchen," she said as she led the way down the hall.

Clay could have found the room by scent alone. The buttery smell of cookies filled the air, drawing him forward until he stopped short in the wide doorway.

Holly was working at the center island. Her dark hair was caught up on top of her head, and several strands had escaped, framing her face. A streak of flour coated one cheek, and she was up to her elbows in cookie dough.

Children stood on chairs around the counter. They formed

a very boisterous, very messy assembly line. One child, the musical Mary Jane, spread a thick layer of frosting on a cookie. She passed it to the next child, who covered the top with sprinkles. The last child carried the colorful treat to an already crowded tray.

"What a wonderful job you guys are doing!" Holly exclaimed. She sprinkled flour onto the counter, picked up a rolling pin, and started rolling out more dough. "What should we make next? Stars, reindeer or Santas?"

When all three children shouted, "Santas!" Clay felt an irrational rush of pride.

Stepping into the kitchen, Eleanor claimed everyone's attention. "Children, we have a visitor." Their gazes focused on Clay, but he was aware only of one stunning pair of emerald eyes. "This is Mr. Clay, a friend of Miss Holly's."

Clay took in the blush staining Holly's fair skin before she ducked her head. She was dressed in a red sweatshirt emblazoned with a snowman, and a pair of jeans. Clay was vaguely aware of the children chiming polite greetings, but only the sound of Holly's voice registered. "What are you doing here, Clay?"

"I heard some of Santa's helpers were making the best cookies in town." He winked at the kids. Then for Holly's benefit, he added, "I couldn't resist."

A little boy carried over a shapeless blob smeared with green frosting and candy sprinkles. "Do you want a Christmas tree?"

"Sure!" Clay took a bite, and the confection crumbled in his mouth, the perfect combination of flaky cookie and sweet frosting. "It's delicious," he told Holly.

She smiled but said, "The kids are the real cooks."

"If you two are all right in here," Eleanor said, "I've some laundry to do while the youngest ones are still down for their naps."

Clay liked how she included him, treating him like he belonged, and responded before Holly had the chance. "We'll be fine."

Eleanor answered with a conspirator's wink and backed out of the kitchen. He had all of two seconds to feel smug before a small, sticky, frosting-coated hand tugged at his. "Do you want to help, Mr. Clay?" Mary Jane asked.

"Um—" *Baking?* He panicked at the thought. He could grill a steak if necessary but…cookies?

"Mr. Forrester isn't here to help us make cookies," Holly answered for him. She lifted an eyebrow, asking, *Why are you here?*

To tell you about the meeting I have planned with Westfell and what it could mean to both our companies' futures. To hear you tell me again that you think I can do this, because, somehow, having you say it is enough to make me believe it.

He wanted to say all that and more, and he wouldn't let a little flour and sugar and…whatever else went into cookies stop him. Unbuttoning his cuffs, Clay rolled up his sleeves. "Miss Holly's right. I didn't come here to make cookies, but since I am here—" he slanted a glance at her "—it's only fair that I pitch in."

One hour and many cookies later, Clay carried the last of the dishes to the sink. "Your elves have abandoned you," he told Holly.

She put away the mixer and looked around the empty kitchen. "They do tend to scatter once cleanup begins."

He turned on the faucet, dumped in some lemony scented dish soap, and raised his voice over the running water. "I guess you're stuck with me."

Despite his teasing tone, Holly regarded him seriously. "What are you doing here, Clay?"

"I went to the flower shop to see you, and Marilyn said you were here, so I thought I'd stop by."

Holly started shaking her head. "I know you mean well, but you can't just show up. The kids might get attached."

"Mary Jane and the other kids took off the minute you told them no more cookies. They're not attached to me. They're attached to desserts."

She ignored him. "I know it's not your intention, but getting close to you is the worst thing that could happen."

Clay shut the water off before she finished speaking, and her last words sounded overly loud in the silence. He noticed Holly didn't mention the children at all in her last statement.

Her eyes pleaded with him, her voice wavering. "They'll get used to seeing you around and start looking forward to your visits. They'll be hurt when you stop coming."

The kids will be hurt, or you will be? Holly certainly knew what the Hopewell kids were going through, but Clay couldn't help thinking she hid her own worries behind her concern for the children. He took two steps, closing the space between them. She didn't retreat, as he'd expected her to. Instead, she stared up at him, her eyes overly bright. He brushed the flour from her cheek, her skin soft beneath his touch.

"It happens at Christmastime." A note of desperation tinged her words. "People want to help, but once the holidays end, they go back to their own lives."

"Is that why you're determined to push me away?"

"Yes. No! I—" Holly caught herself. She lowered her gaze, her eyelashes hiding her eyes. "We were talking about the children."

Clay ran his finger along her jaw, tilting her face toward his. "Were we?"

"Yes," she whispered.

"About how disappointed they'll be if I stop coming."

A childlike vulnerability shone in her eyes, along with feminine desire, the fascinating contradiction so much a part of Holly. "Yes."

"And how it's better not to get too…close." He leaned forward, speaking the words a hairbreadth from her lips.

"Yes."

She moved a mere fraction of an inch; her mouth barely brushed his, but the feather-light touch sent desire spiraling through him. His pulse pounded in his veins, and heat rushed to his groin. The instant response made little sense considering the sweet simplicity of the kiss. But when Holly swayed into him, clinging to his shoulders, Clay didn't give it another thought. He stopped thinking altogether.

Her lips parted, and he couldn't focus on anything other than her exquisite taste. The sugary sweet frosting combined with the feminine flavor that was purely Holly. She circled his tongue with her own, the quick strokes urging him deeper. Swallowing a groan, Clay ran his hands down her sides, to her hips, blindly discovering the curves hidden by her baggy sweat-shirt.

The feel of warm, soft woman hardened his body. In the back of his mind, he knew he and Holly stood in the Hopewell kitchen, that two old ladies and a half a dozen or so children were only a hallway away. This could go no further than a kiss. Even so, he let his mind wander, fantasizing about the delicate skin beneath her clothes.

He imagined cupping her in his hands, and the scent of roses filled his thoughts. A small sound of desire escaped their parted lips, a feminine moan of longing, and arousal flooded his veins. He broke the kiss, nearly gasping for breath, and trailed his lips across her cheek.

"Clay, please." The words broke from Holly in a passion-filled, husky tone that gave away as much as her uneven breathing. "Please stop."

The plea took a long time to register, and part of him, the hard, aching part, thought he'd heard wrong. Resting his forehead against hers, he took a minute to catch his breath.

When he finally lifted his head, he took one look at her flushed face and wide eyes and knew he'd heard right.

Her embarrassed gaze searched the empty kitchen. He easily imagined the scenarios rushing through her mind. Impressionable children, old-fashioned ladies. What if someone had walked in?

"Holly," he said, his voice rougher than he intended, "nothing happened."

She shot him a disbelieving look, and he regretted his choice of words as she backed out of his arms. "I mean, *something* happened. We kissed. But no one's lurking in the pantry, waiting to jump out at us."

"I know. It's just that you make me…" Her words trailed off, but Clay couldn't let that go.

"I make you what?" he asked, curious to hear her describe their incredible chemistry.

"Forget," she said finally.

Frowning, he echoed, "I make you forget?"

She nodded. "I should know better, but you make me forget the lessons I've learned."

She'd all but spelled out those lessons before he kissed her. Lessons of disappointment and heartache. Lessons that had taught her not to let anyone too close.

"Maybe that's not such a bad thing."

Sadness tinged her smile. "Maybe not. But it's hard to forget who you are. Or, in my case, who I'm not."

She lost him with that statement. Clay didn't know much about who she wasn't; he knew who she was. She was sweet, loving, vulnerable, and she awakened protective instincts he'd never realized he possessed. "Holly—"

He didn't have the chance say more. "Holly, dear?" Eleanor's voice echoed his through the closed kitchen door. By the time the older woman entered the kitchen, he and Holly stood side by side, doing the dishes. "Holly, Catherine Hopkins is here. I thought you might want to say hello."

Holly's hands stilled in the dishwater. She cleared her throat. "Of course." Reaching for a dish towel, she explained to Clay, "Catherine's a caseworker for some of the children here. I'll be right back."

After the two women left the kitchen, Clay finished doing the last of the dishes. The monotonous chore kept his hands busy but failed to occupy his mind. All he could think about was the hurt Holly hoped to avoid by isolating herself. The idea of a woman as giving, as loving, as Holly locking her heart away to keep it safe sent a swift kick of denial to his gut.

It wasn't right. She should be able to trust her heart, to know that he would never hurt her—

Wait, what was he thinking? That he could be the man to undo the damage those hard-learned lessons had caused?

Not likely. His ex-wife had told him more than once during their marriage exactly what he had to offer a woman. He was rich, good-looking and great in bed. But when it came to *being there,* when it came to *understanding,* Victoria had made it equally plain he failed.

He hadn't bothered to defend himself. And there were some mistakes a man didn't repeat.

No, he had to get out before he got in too deep. Drying his hands with quick, rough movements, he ignored the voice that asked if it wasn't already too late.

He entered the hall, and female voices drifted toward him from the foyer. "There's still no word about Lucas's family?" Holly asked.

"Nothing so far. His mother said the father wasn't involved with Lucas, but now that she's disappeared, it's hard to know if what she said was true."

"I don't suppose…if you'd heard anything…" The hesitancy in Holly's voice carried down the hall, as did the social worker's sympathy.

"Believe me, Holly, I wouldn't bother with small talk if I'd heard that you'd been approved to adopt Lucas. Those would be the first words out of my mouth."

"I know," Holly admitted, with a shaky laugh. "It's so hard to wait when all I want to do is take Lucas home."

The door opened, and Clay heard Holly bid the other woman goodbye. Despite his intent to leave, he quietly backed toward the kitchen. He didn't want Holly to know he'd overheard her conversation.

Holly would be an amazing mother, and after what he'd learned about her childhood, he wasn't surprised she wanted to save a child from that same lonely fate. No doubt she would shower Lucas with love.

An image sprang to mind of Holly smiling, her green eyes sparkling as she took Lucas to the park, dressed him for school or tucked the boy into bed. Everyday, normal tasks that she would never take for granted.

It was all too easy to picture, and the longer he imagined the scenes, the more details his mind provided. The scent of fresh-cut grass at the park; the taste of old-fashioned peanut butter and jelly sandwiches, which Holly would pack for the little boy's lunch; the sweet sound of her voice as she sang him to sleep.

Clay could see it all. More than that, as the mental camera zoomed out and broadened those pictures, he saw himself at Holly's side in every shot.

The thought startled him, and he barely managed a response as Sylvia Hopewell stepped into the kitchen. "Mr. Forrester, I'd gone out for errands after lunch and was so pleased when my sister told me you were here."

With those pictures of Holly and Lucas—and *him*—still swirling in full color in his mind, Clay struggled to find a smile. "I came by to see Holly and couldn't resist the lure of sugar cookies."

"Ah, yes. Nothing else tastes so much like Christmas," she mused. "How my sister and I loved those when we were growing up!"

Had any of Holly's foster parents bothered with Christmas traditions? Clay wondered. Could you even *have* a tradition when every year might mean a new "family" and a new home? No doubt Holly hoped to spare Lucas that kind of an empty childhood.

"Such wonderful memories." Sylvia gave a melancholy sigh. "That's the gift Eleanor and I hope to have given all the children who've passed through our home." Brushing a fingertip beneath her glasses, she said, "Ah, forgive me, Mr. Forrester. It's been an emotional time for all of us."

A bad feeling wormed its way through Clay's stomach. "Are you and Eleanor all right?"

"Oh, yes, we're fine. It's nothing like that, thank goodness. No, it's the house." Reaching out, she ran a hand along the counter, the shine of tears coming to her eyes. "In just a few weeks, Hopewell House will be closing."

Chapter Six

"You can't close the house," Clay burst out, looking around for any sign that the house would be closing and not finding any. "If it's a matter of needing more help or money—"

"It isn't that. You're so kind to offer, but I'm afraid it's too late."

Too late? "What will happen to the children?"

"They'll be sent to different foster homes," Sylvia explained, her typical smile taking a downward turn. "The arrangements have been made, but we've put off moving the children until after the holidays to give us all a last Christmas together. And delaying the inevitable, I suppose." She sighed. "You'd think after all these years we'd be ready for goodbye. Of course, I always thought we'd have a say in the matter."

"You're being forced out?" Clay demanded, anger burning in his gut. How could anyone think of separating the children from each other? And from Holly.

Sylvia lifted her hands helplessly. "It's the house. It bears our name, but it isn't ours. We leased it from a wealthy family, but the original owner recently passed away, and his grandson sold the house to a property management company."

"Property management?" he echoed.

"Yes, Hendrix Properties."

The words sounded like a death knell, and his righteous anger soured into guilt. Thanks to some sound business advice and an influx of cash, the once struggling company, which had handled business properties, had started purchasing residential homes. Due to the high costs of real estate, the profit-margin turnaround for converting large older homes into multifamily rentals promised to make Kevin Hendrix a wealthy man.

Clay would know. *He'd* been the one to give the advice, the one to invest the cash, and he, too, had been counting on making money on the deal.

"Mr. Forrester?" The older woman watched him, concern in her kind eyes. "Are you all right?"

Clay forced himself to nod. "I'm fine."

But as Sylvia left to help Eleanor, he looked around the cozy kitchen that had welcomed so many lost souls and knew he was far from fine.

A few minutes later, the kitchen door opened, and Holly stepped inside. Knowing what he'd done, he could barely meet her eyes. But in the brief glance, he saw the toll the conversation with Catherine had taken. Holly's eyes had lost their sparkle, and a tired frown lined her forehead.

"Sorry about that," she said.

Clay stayed silent, not even knowing where to start. He longed to ask Holly about her desire to adopt Lucas, but that was information he wasn't supposed to know. He longed to kiss away the troubled frown and rekindle the smile that had lit her face as she'd helped the children. But how hypocritical was that when he was partly responsible for the house's impending closure?

"Holly," he began, but the confession stalled in his throat. Still coming to grips with the realization, he couldn't bring himself to tell her.

With a questioning glance, she said, "You never did say why you stopped by."

Grimacing, he thought of his smug satisfaction, his certainty that he'd found a way to change the company's philosophy. The sweet taste of success had turned to ash. He'd been so focused on righting his father's wrongs. Who was going to fix *his* mistake?

"I, um, came by to thank you. What you said at lunch made me realize I was holding on to the past."

"Really?" Surprise lit her eyes. "I did that?"

"Yeah, you did that," Clay told her, his voice gruff. "You're an amazing woman, Holly."

Soft color brightened her cheeks. "I'm glad to help, but I'm not sure I made that much of a difference."

"Thanks to you, I realized I couldn't just change one corner of the business and expect everything else to fall into place. To be effective, I really have to commit, even if that means losing an employee."

Holly winced. "Someone quit?"

"Yeah. Albert Jensen. You met him at the party. He was my father's best friend."

"I'm sorry. I hate to think of anyone losing his job."

How like Holly to care about a person she didn't know. Jensen hadn't blinked at the hundreds of JW Shipping employees who would have lost their jobs thanks to him. Kevin Hendrix probably hadn't given a second thought to the children he was evicting.

God, he had to fix this! But how?

"I was talking to Sylvia." The next words nearly lodged in his throat, but not saying them wouldn't make them any less true. "She told me how they're being forced to close the house."

Sorrow bowed Holly's shoulders, and Clay wished he hadn't said a word. But if he was going to help the Hopewell sisters, he needed to know what Kevin Hendrix had done. What he, Clay, had helped him do.

"The Hopewells started taking in children thirty years ago. They've done so much good here. But, somehow, the owner doesn't see things as I do."

The confusion in her gaze revealed Holly's innocence and the purity of her heart. A logical businessman, like Kevin Hendrix, like Clay's father, would formulate a logical, business-minded answer. But Holly didn't think with her wallet; she thought with her heart.

"You've talked to Kevin Hendrix?" he asked.

"I called him, for all the good it did," she said bitterly. "He said he was sorry, but I shouldn't take it personally. It was business, and if he hadn't bought the house, someone else would have. As if that made it okay."

Jensen had argued that same point; thanks to Holly's encouragement, Clay had stood up to his father's former right-hand man. Too bad he hadn't done that when Kevin Hendrix came to him.

Clay thought back to his own meeting with Hendrix. He'd jumped on Clay's suggest to diversify the business from strictly commercial property renovations to residential. Of course, Clay's plan—and infusion of cash—was the only thing keeping Hendrix's company from bankruptcy, but Clay had been impressed by the other man's willingness to embrace the new idea.

"I found the perfect house! An enormous brownstone that will easily convert into four separate units. The guy who owns it inherited the place from his grandfather, but between the inheritance tax, property tax, and upkeep on the place, he can't wait to sell."

Clay had listened with a sense of satisfaction. Finally, he'd found a way to make a profit without profiting from another company's loss. "Sounds perfect, Kevin."

The pause from the other man should have told him no deal was *that* perfect. "There are some renters in the house now, but—"

"But what?"

"Nothing," Kevin had reassured him. "I'll take care of it."

With a sick feeling in his stomach, Clay now knew how the other man had taken care of things. He should have asked what Kevin planned, but he didn't. Should have asked about the people living in the house, but he didn't. Instead, he'd set his sights on what he wanted and gone after it. He'd kept his focus strictly on business.

Just like his father.

"Holly, I—I have to go. There's something I have to do."

Startled by the sudden announcement, Holly blinked. "Oh, sure, of course. You're busy. You've got more important—"

"No." He silenced her with a quick kiss. Nothing was more important than Holly, the foster home, and reversing the damage he'd caused. "Not more important. Just something I need to take care of. I'll call you later."

"Clay." Uncertainty rang in her voice, and she caught her lower lip between her teeth.

Backing out of the kitchen, he repeated, "I'll call you."

But not, he silently vowed, until he'd found a way to fix what he'd done.

Holly took a final swipe at the already clean butcher-block counter. The older kids had settled down for an afternoon nap, giving the adults a chance to rest. The lingering smell of sugar cookies combined with the cinnamon tea brewing on the stove.

"Take a seat," Eleanor urged as she poured two steaming

cups. "Haven't you figured out yet that rest time for the children is simply an excuse for us adults to sit a spell?"

Accepting the tea, Holly joined the older woman at the table. Five years ago, when Holly wanted to find a way to help children lost and alone in the foster system like she had been, she'd found Hopewell House. But she quickly realized she gained as much from her time volunteering there as the children did. Hopewell House had become her haven, the only place where she truly belonged. With the group home closing soon, she wanted to spend every spare moment soaking up the love the Hopewell sisters offered to every soul who passed through their doors.

But now, everywhere she looked, Holly saw Clay. Dressed in a Santa suit, passing out presents, teasing her about her own Christmas wish. Standing at the island, eating cookies and praising the kids' messy but enthusiastic efforts. Pressing her up against the counter and kissing her until her legs went weak.

Eleanor peered at Holly over the rim of her delicate floral teacup. "It was quite a surprise for Mr. Forrester to drop by, wasn't it?"

Trying not to put even greater emphasis on Clay showing up, out of the blue, again, Holly murmured, "You know how it is this time of year. Holiday spirit and all."

"Right. Because that's how all wealthy businessmen donate their time and talents." The teacup wasn't large enough to hide Eleanor's smile. "By frosting sugar cookies."

Busted, Holly thought and gave a short laugh. She knew Eleanor had a type of ESP when it came to the children. Evidently, that ability also extended to adults. "Doesn't anyone ever get away with anything around here?"

"Never," the woman declared and chuckled. "And believe me, they've tried. Now, no matter how wonderful he is with the children, why won't you admit Clay's real interest is in you?"

"Why would a man like Clay Forrester be interested in a nobody like me?"

"Why on earth wouldn't he be?" Eleanor demanded.

Holly shrugged. "It's not like we have anything in common."

"So, the two of you have nothing to talk about? You're completely bored with each other?"

Bored. Not likely. The very thought of him sent her pulse racing. And it wasn't just his sexy smile, startling blue eyes, or his eye-catching build. He challenged her preconceptions of rich businessmen with his compassion and intrigued her with his determination to change the way his company operated. Not even a lifetime with Clay would leave her feeling bored.

A lifetime…

Holly shoved that thought right out of her head. Neither of them was interested in that level of commitment. He had a business to turn around and a bad marriage behind him, while she, well, she wasn't going to take that kind of chance on a relationship again. She'd learned that opening her heart led only to disappointment.

She still remembered the night she told Mark about her childhood. Listening to her pour her heart out, he'd sympathized with her loneliness, her disappointment, her feeling of never belonging. He'd acted so concerned, so caring, and she'd fallen for it, even his hokey line that she didn't have to worry about being alone anymore.

They'd made love for the first time that night, but Holly refused to blame Mark for taking advantage. She'd *given* him the advantage by foolishly trusting him.

But it quickly became obvious Mark's caring and concern had more to do with *Mark* than it did with her. He refused her offers to visit Hopewell House and disapproved of the time she spent there, yet made it seem like his protests were for her own good.

"You should leave your years in foster homes in the past. All the time you spend at that place makes it harder for you to move on."

She'd even bought his line for a while, only to realize she couldn't stay away. Her time at Hopewell House filled an emptiness inside that her relationship with Mark never touched.

An emptiness she rarely noticed when she was with the kids…or with Clay. Forced to admit the truth, she said, "No, Clay's definitely not boring, but he's—"

"He's not Mark," Eleanor said softly.

"I know that." The response came automatically, but no matter how wonderful Clay was, she couldn't imagine he'd react any differently to her desire to foster Lucas.

As if reading Holly's thoughts, Eleanor said, "I've seen a great many triumphs and tragedies in the foster system. I've seen how hard it is when someone you love disappoints you. But if you stop believing in people, the only one you're disappointing is yourself."

"This has got to work," Clay muttered, lifting the receiver and punching in a number.

The information he'd collected on Hopewell House lay on his desk along with the existing file for Hendrix Properties. He'd memorized every minute detail, including the most pressing point—the deadline for shutting down the foster home.

Guilt pressed on his chest, the weight of his conscience nearly enough to suffocate him. Picturing Holly's green eyes filled with tears as the foster home's doors closed forever, Clay knew he had to do anything in his power to keep that from happening.

He *had* to fix this!

Showing up at the house, dressed as Santa Claus, he'd pictured himself as some kind of hero, wanting to prove to

Holly he wasn't the ruthless man she thought him to be. If she knew the truth—

Clay cut the thought off; somehow, he was going to fix this.

One hour and numerous phone calls later, he dialed the number to Hopewell House. Barely able to contain his excitement, he waited impatiently for one of the Hopewell sisters to answer.

"Hopewell House."

"Eleanor, it's Clay Forrester. I have wonderful news."

The older woman's laughter filled the line. "Mr. Forrester, you are certainly full of surprises. I must say, this Christmas has meant as much to my sister and me as it has to the children. Most of that is thanks to you."

Desperately wanting that to be true, he said, "I hope to make this a Christmas for all of you to remember. I've found another house."

"A house?"

"It's larger than the one you have now, and best of all, my company will donate its use. You won't ever have to worry about losing—"

"Mr. Forrester," Eleanor interrupted gently, "I cannot thank you enough for what you've done. Not just the gifts, but also the time and the attention you've given us."

"I haven't done much." Guilt squirmed in his stomach. "Believe me." It wasn't nearly enough. Unless he could fix what he'd done, it would never be enough. "But this house I've found, it's perfect."

"The house and your generosity are amazing. Unfortunately, it isn't just about losing the house. Not anymore." She sighed. "Once my sister and I realized we couldn't keep Hopewell House open, we took it as a sign that it was time for us to retire. After all, we've been fostering children for thirty years."

"I know all the good you've done, and with this new house, you can keep doing that work—"

"Mr. Forrester, even if Sylvia and I hadn't decided to retire, permits for a new home would take weeks, if not longer. New foster homes have already been found for most of the children, and the rest will be placed soon. It's simply too late to keep the children together."

Barely registering Eleanor's quiet thanks and farewell, Clay hung up the phone.

Too late.

If only he'd known about Hopewell House sooner. If only he'd learned about it before the children had been reassigned, before the Hopewells had made their plans for retirement. But he hadn't known, and the one question he dreaded to ask, the one answer he feared to face, remained.

If he hadn't met Holly, if he hadn't been inspired by her love for the children, would he have cared about the house's closing?

Holly's heart pounded recklessly as the elevator rose toward Clay's office. If she'd raced up all thirty flights of stairs, she didn't think it would beat much harder. She knew how busy he was, but once Eleanor called, Holly had rushed to see him.

"That man is incredible," Eleanor had stated the moment Holly picked up the phone.

She hadn't needed to ask whom the older woman was referring to. After all, Clay was the most incredible man she'd ever met. But Eleanor's words proved he was more than Holly could have imagined.

It was time to face the truth. Clay was nothing like Mark. Instead, he was a wonderful man who was attracted to her. Possibly as attracted as she was to him.

As she waited impatiently for the elevator doors to open, Holly vowed to stop looking beyond that attraction. To stop looking for trouble where none existed. The differences in their lives remained, and she knew she would never find a permanent place in his world. But no one said their relationship had to be about forever. Not as long as they were both willing to live for the moment.

The elevator doors slid open, and Holly stepped out. She flashed a smile at Marie. "Is Clay busy? I know I should have called, but—"

His assistant waved off her apology and stood. "I wouldn't have had the chance to put you through. He's been burning up the phone lines all morning."

Holly's heart fell. Disappointed, she said, "I'll come back later."

"No, this is perfect," Marie said as she caught Holly's arm and led the way toward Clay's office. "He needs to take a break, and this way he has no excuse." Marie knocked on the door and shoved it open. In an exaggerated whisper, she said, "Holly's here to see you."

As if he couldn't see that for himself, Holly thought, with embarrassment, as Marie waved her inside and shut the door.

"I'll have to call you back," Clay said into the phone as she walked toward his desk.

Clearly, Marie hadn't exaggerated about his hectic day. He'd abandoned his jacket and shoved his shirtsleeves back unevenly, one above the elbow, the other up to his muscled forearm. His tie had been pulled free, and his usually neat dark hair spilled over his forehead.

As he listened to whoever was on the other end of the line, his gaze never left her face. A ripple of anticipation stole through Holly. She'd never seen him look so serious, so focused, so…sexy.

It was as if her decision to accept the attraction between them, and follow where it led, had opened her eyes to just how handsome Clay truly was. Little wonder that the rest of her senses joined in. His rich baritone sent chills running down her spine, and her fingertips itched to smooth away his troubled frown.

After hanging up the phone, Clay pushed away from his desk, the wheels crinkling against the protective paper covering the carpeting. "Holly. I wasn't expecting you."

Her heart picked up its pace as he circled the desk. Was he going to kiss her again? she wondered. Another bone-melting kiss would go a long way to reassure her she was doing the right thing. He stopped mere inches away, close enough for her to feel his body heat, close enough to leave her helplessly leaning toward him.

But when his frown didn't fade, she stepped back, needing the breathing room as she stumbled to explain. "You're busy. I told Marie I could come back later."

"No, wait." Reaching out, he caught her hand. Not the passionate embrace she'd hoped for but enough to stop her from easing toward the exit. "I need to talk to you. I'd just hoped for better news," he muttered.

"Clay, it's okay." Linking their fingers, she gave a grateful squeeze. "I know about Hopewell House."

His throat moved as he swallowed. "You do?"

"Eleanor told me how you offered them a new house. That's the most amazing thing anyone has ever done."

Clay flinched, and to her surprise, the tension straining his features tightened. "Holly, you don't understand."

Thinking he considered his efforts a failure, she told him, "I know it's too late to keep the kids together, but that you even tried…"

Words escaped her as she tried to capture the emotions. Unable to give a verbal explanation, Holly curved a hand behind his neck and drew his head down. The warm puff of his breath teased her lips; then his mouth was there, warm and wonderful against her own, but something was missing.

Unlike with their other kisses, when Holly had followed where Clay had led, he seemed oddly restrained. He stood still as stone, with his hands fisted at his sides. Greedy for the passion he'd given before, she brushed aside his resistance with the stroke of her tongue, the gentle nip of her teeth against his lower lip. He shuddered and, with a groan of surrender, pulled her tightly into his arms. Her heart did a wild victory dance as she explored the heat and muscle of his shoulders and back.

Passion shimmered inside her, amplifying every touch until the stroke of Clay's fingers against her spine and the heat of his palm at her hip sent shivers racing through her. She felt dizzy, light-headed, as he stole her breath and, she feared, her soul.

Finally, Clay lifted his head, breaking the kiss. Their heavy breathing filled the air, the needy, rapid sound adding to the crackling tension. Holly didn't want to stop, but her focus widened slightly, beyond the intimate scope of Clay's arms, and she recalled she'd interrupted him at work.

A little embarrassed that she'd gotten so carried away, she said, "When Eleanor told me what you'd done, I had to thank you."

Closing his eyes, he rested his forehead against hers. "What I did…I wanted to fix this. I know how much Hopewell House means to you."

The certainty and the anguish in his tone made her ask, "The sisters told you about my childhood, didn't they?"

"Eleanor did, but I'm sure she didn't mean to break a confidence."

Holly shook her head. "It's okay. It's not a secret."

"Do you want to tell me about it?" Clay asked. Sympathy and that lingering look—of guilt?—still darkened his expression, but his gentle touch as he brushed a lock of hair from her still-heated cheek encouraged her. She let him lead her to the plastic-covered couch, pondering his question.

Did she want to tell Clay about her childhood? Was it some kind of test, to see if he passed where Mark had so miserably failed? Or was it something she wanted to share, the way he'd shared his goal of changing the family business?

If you stop believing in people, the only one you're disappointing is yourself. As usual, Eleanor was right.

Tucked against his side, with his arm draped over her shoulders, Holly still felt the heat of attraction, but it was mellower now, a banked fire rather than an inferno. "What do you want to know?"

"Do you know anything about your biological parents?"

"Very little," she said.

When she was younger, she'd tried to envision them, tried to imagine how life with them might have been. But it had been like staring into a dark void. She had no frame of reference, no landmarks to guide her, no true connection to another living soul.

"Next to nothing about my biological father," Holly added. "My mother was sixteen, and she signed the papers putting me up for adoption before I was born."

"But you weren't adopted?"

"I was premature. I was in and out of hospitals and considered a high risk. My health improved as I grew older, but older kids are harder to place. Then, when I was five…" Swallowing against the ache in her throat, Holly was surprised that telling the old story still caused such a feeling of loss. "There was a couple, the Parkers. They came for visits, and we went to the park and the zoo. I was old enough to know what those visits meant."

She could still remember the childish but desperate desire to please her prospective parents. If she was good enough, pretty enough, smart enough, maybe, just maybe, they would like her enough.

"What happened?" Clay asked softly.

Lifting her head, Holly looked up at him. Wrapped in the compassion of his gaze, she found the strength to finish the story. "Before the adoption went through, Mrs. Parker got pregnant. They'd been trying for years, and with their own child on the way, they decided against adoption."

"Holly, I'm so sorry." Clay stroked the soft curve of her cheek, struggling not to reveal the battle with his conscience.

He couldn't tell Holly that his company was the driving force behind Hopewell House closing. Not yet, and certainly not now. Not after the heart-wrenching story she'd just told. All she'd ever wanted was a home and family, and the Hopewell sisters and the foster kids were as close as she'd come.

Admitting what he'd done would be the same as admitting defeat, and Clay wasn't about to give up. Somehow he would make this right.

"Clay, it's okay," Holly whispered.

He tried to rub away the frown furrowing his forehead and ease the tension tightening his shoulders. That she would even try to console *him* sent another shaft of guilt to pierce his heart.

"It was a long time ago," she added.

"But the hurt is still there."

"With Hopewell House closing and…everything, all these memories and emotions feel so raw, like it's happening all over again."

Clay knew that Lucas was the *everything* Holly spoke of. No wonder those old wounds seemed fresh. Once again, she was playing the waiting game after trying to prove she was *good enough* to be Lucas's foster mother. Why hadn't the agency instantly approved Holly? Anyone who spent five minutes with her and Lucas could see how much she loved him, could see what a perfect mother she would be.

"Holly—" Clay cut himself off. She didn't know he'd overheard her conversation with the caseworker. He sensed she'd been careful *not* to reveal her desire to foster the little boy.

Did she think he wouldn't understand? he wondered, with

something that felt like hurt. He understood perfectly and wished…what? That she would trust him? He was the last person to deserve her trust.

Lifting a hand, she touched his jaw. The desire he'd been fighting since she'd stolen his breath with that amazing kiss rushed through his veins, multiplying his guilt. If Holly knew what he'd done…

As she gazed up at him with wide, innocent eyes, she whispered, "Thank you."

"Don't, Holly. I'm not—"

"You're a wonderful man." A rosy blush tinted her cheeks, as if she hadn't meant to say the words out loud.

The sudden beep of the intercom startled them both and saved Clay from another round of guilt. "What is it, Marie?" he called, gruffly clearing his throat.

"Sorry to interrupt," she said through the speaker, "but this afternoon's conference call is on line two."

"I have to take that," he told Holly, reluctance and relief blending together in a confusing mix.

"Of course. I mean, you're at work." Still looking flustered, she stood.

Her lips were still pink and slightly swollen. Her hair was tousled; the collar of her pale blue sweater, crooked. All telltale signs of their unexpected make-out session, each a temptation to pull her back into his arms.

No, Clay thought fiercely, he couldn't do it. He shoved his fists into his pockets, denying the temptation. No matter how much he wanted Holly, he had to keep his distance until he fixed what he'd done or until he came clean.

"Um, I was thinking—" Holly tugged at the hem of her sweater, trying to straighten it, but the collar remained adorably crooked "—maybe I could fix dinner for you at my place tonight."

The offer of dinner barely registered, his focus centered on the idea of being alone with Holly at her apartment. Not a good idea if he intended to keep the vow he'd made, but one look at her hopeful expression shook his determination to keep his distance.

"Actually, Holly…" he began.

She must have heard the regret in his voice, because the hope in her eyes instantly died. "It's okay. I understand. Really. I didn't mean to dump all over you." Without making eye contact, she started for the door. "Thank you again for all you've done."

"Holly, wait."

He couldn't do it. He couldn't let her leave, thinking that what she'd revealed about her childhood had made a difference. "I have a family get-together tonight. How about a movie tomorrow instead?"

"That would be great." Her pleased smile would make torture worthwhile.

And torture, Clay decided, was exactly what his no-touch policy would be. Still, it was just a movie. Sitting side by side in a theater, certainly he'd be able to keep his hands to himself.

Chapter Seven

"And now, for the crowning touch." Clay slipped the angel on top of the tree and climbed down from the stepladder in the center of his mother's parlor. "Next year we get a tree no taller than I am!"

A chorus of boos sounded from his nephews, thanks to some encouragement from his sister, Anne. She and her two boys had handled decorating the lower branches, while Clay had been responsible for the top half. As a result, wooden ornaments and homemade decorations dotted the bottom of the tree, while delicate glass balls and treasured keepsakes hung from the top.

It wasn't an aesthetically perfect tree, like those in the years before his nephews were born. Back then, the white lights, glittering gold balls and artfully placed bows had blended beautifully with the parlor's soft hues and ivory brocade furniture. The entire room had had a sterile, museum-like feel.

Clay decided he'd take a hodgepodge tree and the boisterous laughter of his nephews any day.

"The tree looks wonderful."

Glancing over his shoulder at his mother, Clay gave an encouraging smile. Petite and blond, wearing an off-white silk pantsuit, Jillian Forrester was as stylish and lovely as ever, despite the sadness shadowing her eyes.

He knew how difficult Christmas was for her. Bittersweet memories were unwrapped with every ornament. His mother wanted to forgo the yearly tree raising, but Clay wouldn't let her. As a family, they needed to establish new traditions, new memories, and Anne's two energetic boys were a big help in lightening the mood.

"We have chocolate chip cookies for dessert," Jillian announced. "But…" Catching the boys by the shoulder as they ran toward the kitchen, she added, "I think it's only fair that Uncle Clay gets first choice since he set up the tree."

The boys groaned, and Clay laughed. "Sounds good to me. And, man, am I hungry. I might eat the whole batch!"

The protests grew louder, and Anne shook her head. "Sometimes I think you're as immature as Shawn."

"I try my best."

After Jillian herded her grandsons into the kitchen, Anne said to Clay, "Thanks for setting up the tree. It means so much to Mother."

"I wouldn't miss it," he said, meaning the words, even though thoughts of Holly had distracted him all day, stealing his attention away from his family.

Every small show of affection Anne lavished on her boys brought an image of Holly and Lucas to mind. He could picture her admiring a handmade ornament, stuffing stockings with gifts, or capturing each moment on film. But just like the day at Hopewell House, he kept insinuating himself into Holly's dream and seeing her *here,* with his family—a part of his family.

The whole idea was crazy… So why did it feel so right?

"Clay, are you okay?" his sister asked as she caught him standing still, a forgotten box of unused ornaments in hand.

"Yeah, sure," he replied, setting the box aside and folding up the stepladder.

Eying him closely, Anne echoed, "Yeah, sure."

It took a moment for Clay to hear the sarcasm in his sister's voice. "What?"

"Something is going on with you. Is there a problem with the company?"

Clay gave a short laugh. For the first time in over a year, the family business *wasn't* filling his thoughts. "Nothing more than usual," he said, refusing to bring up Jensen's resignation.

"Dad knew what he was doing when he left the business to you."

Clay wasn't so sure. "Maybe he should have left you in charge. You are the firstborn."

She snorted. "Yeah, but I'm just a girl."

"A girl with an MBA," Clay added, even though their father had often overlooked that accomplishment. He'd been far more impressed with Anne's marriage to a prominent sportscaster and the birth of her two sons.

Anne shrugged. "Book smart doesn't equal business smart, or so Dad always said." With a touch of unusual self-consciousness, she added, "I'm considering putting his theory to the test."

"You're looking for a job?" Clay asked, then hoped the question hadn't sounded as incredulous to Anne as it had to him.

"Now that Shawn's in kindergarten, I don't need to be home all day. Anyway, it was just a thought." She gave a short laugh. "I'll probably find out I don't have what it takes to make it in the business world."

"You can do anything you put your mind to, Anne. Don't doubt it for a second."

"Uncle Clay!" Bobby rushed in from the kitchen, his

freckled face smudged with chocolate and a second cookie clenched in his hand. "Gramma said Shawn and me could have two cookies. We took the biggest ones!"

"Hey, no fair! Your grandma said I got first choice."

"You were too slow, so now we're gonna eat 'em all!"

"No, you are not," Anne told her older son. Shooting Clay a scolding look, she murmured, "See what you started?"

"He's your kid. You can tell by the love of chocolate and the appalling manners."

Ignoring him, Anne knelt down and wiped the spot of chocolate from the corner of her son's mouth. "I know Grandma said you could have two cookies, but I don't think she'd want you eating in here. Go finish that in the kitchen, and tell Shawn that two means two. Not four or six, or however many he's stuffed into his pockets."

Bobby nodded, his dark bangs flapping against his forehead, and raced for the kitchen. Watching the little boy, Clay wasn't sure what to make of the funny catch in his chest. "You're a great mother, Annie."

His sister blinked, startled either by the compliment or the use of her childhood nickname. "Thank you."

Clay always enjoyed time spent with his family, but since meeting Holly, he'd realized just how lucky he was. She'd never felt the support and acceptance he'd always taken for granted. It made the love she showered on Lucas and the rest of the kids at Hopewell House even more amazing.

Anne stared at her brother. "Okay, who is she?"

"What?"

"If it's not business on your mind, then it must be personal. So who is she?"

"I have met someone," he admitted. He thought of Holly's smile, her giving spirit, her capacity for love despite the loneliness of her childhood. "Someone special."

But despite the way his mind kept playing tricks on him,

superimposing his presence on a future with Holly and Lucas, Clay couldn't consider that future until he made up for the past—his father's and his own.

And even then…the thought of falling in love again and banking on that fragile emotion didn't seem worth the risk. Especially if it meant failing a second time and finding out Victoria was right: he couldn't give enough of himself to make a woman happy.

Her eyes alight, Anne threw her arms around his shoulders. "Oh, my gosh! That's great. Mom and I have been so worried."

"Whoa. Take it easy. And why were you worried?"

Stepping back, his sister said, "About the way you acted after the divorce. You've always been a responsible guy, but you shouldn't have taken full blame for the trouble in your marriage."

He'd shouldered the blame because he'd been the one at fault. He'd let himself get distracted by work, burying his head in business rather than facing the problems in their relationship, problems that had existed from the start.

Victoria had married him because he could offer her a certain lifestyle. She'd wanted to live well and party hard and marry a man with a name and social position equal to her own. He'd given her that, but she'd always had an indefinable need for more. His time, his attention, his love, no matter how much he tried to give, none of it had been enough.

"I couldn't make her happy."

Anne rolled her eyes. "No one could make Victoria happy. As much as I hate how she treated you, I can't help feeling sorry for her."

"I wouldn't waste too many tears. Last I heard, she was seeing some hotshot movie producer."

"Big deal. I can guarantee she's still miserable."

"I'm not so sure, Anne. I think the divorce pretty much did the trick."

His sister's eyes widened. "See? That's what I'm talking

about. *You're* not the reason Victoria's unhappy. I meant she's still miserable because she's still, well, Victoria. She's spoiled, selfish, and she's unhappy with everything and everyone because she's unhappy with herself. It has *nothing* to do with you."

The sincerity in Anne's expression made Clay want to believe that with Holly things could be different. That they could be happy together and he could be there for Holly in the way he'd failed Victoria.

But while he agreed Victoria was spoiled and selfish, Anne had it wrong about his marriage. Victoria had made it more than clear he'd been the cause of her misery.

"No, no, no!" Holly gazed anxiously in the mirror at her naked face and unstyled hair. Six-forty. She'd figured Clay would be prompt, but certainly a man with his dating experience knew better than to show up for a date twenty minutes early!

The doorbell pealed again, and Holly knew she had no choice but to suffer the embarrassment of opening the door looking less than her best. So much for wowing him with her appearance, she thought as she walked to the front door.

"I am so not ready, but that's your…"

Her words cut off as she opened the door. Instead of Clay, Catherine Hopkins stood in the hallway. Holly had known the caseworker for years, thanks to her time at Hopewell House, but their relationship certainly didn't include unannounced visits at home.

To anyone else, the woman's face might have been poker ready, but Holly knew better. She'd been at Hopewell House on a day when the courts remanded a little boy to the custody of his family, even though everyone, everyone, knew of the physical abuse going on. She'd seen Catherine's face that day. Her expression then mirrored the look Holly saw now…and she knew.

"They turned me down." Even as she spoke the words, Holly couldn't seem to process them. "They turned me down."

"Holly, I'm so sorry." Catherine tipped her hand as she took a step inside the apartment. "I know how much you love Lucas. No one can deny that."

"I think they just did," she said, with a disbelieving laugh, which covered a sob building in her throat.

"You have to understand. The agency wasn't sure you could care for Lucas on a full-time basis. You work forty hours a week. You're single. You're so young...."

Catherine's words trailed off, and Holly wondered if she'd picked up on the same irony. As a child, she'd been told she was too old for adoption and now... "I'm too young?"

If they had any idea how old she felt...

In the years she'd volunteered at Hopewell House, Holly had grown accustomed to children coming and going. She'd learned to love them all while carefully keeping herself from becoming attached, but with Lucas, her detachment had crumbled the moment she saw him.

Catherine had brought him to Hopewell House on a crisp spring day. Holly had walked out with Eleanor to greet the caseworker. Standing beside the car, Catherine and Eleanor had discussed Lucas's missing mother, but Holly had been drawn to the back window.

An angel slept in the car seat. Tousled blond curls capped a round, red-cheeked face. The toddler was asleep, but his mouth still worked as he sucked on his thumb. As she watched, his pale lashes fluttered, his eyes opened, and their eyes met. Even with the car door closed, she could hear the word he mouthed around his thumb. "Mama."

Lucas had only been two at the time, with a toddler's limited vocabulary. Still, she'd never forgotten that moment. Even in the following months, when Lucas started calling her Miss Holly, as all the children did, she'd still felt that special bond.

"I know it probably doesn't mean much," Catherine said, "but I vouched for you…for all the good it did."

Holly knew she should thank the woman for her efforts—manners ingrained in her by some long-forgotten, ever-changing foster family—but the words caught on the lump in her throat.

"The Hopewell sisters want you to call them."

Holly managed a brief nod as the woman slowly backed out of the apartment. The sisters had supported her emotionally for years, but soon they would be leaving, moving half a country away, and she'd be alone again.

It was nothing new, the loneliness, the disappointment, but oh, how it hurt! Tears burned her eyes, her throat, her soul as she sank down against the door Catherine had closed behind her. A door that had been slammed shut on her life as Lucas's foster mother.

A broken sob escaped. The sound seemed to echo in the empty apartment. Only instead of fading away, the sound grew louder, more ragged and wrenching, until Holly realized she couldn't stop the sobs bursting from her chest.

She had known the cards were stacked against her, had known all the reasons why she might not be approved to foster Lucas. But she'd let herself believe she stood a chance, convinced love counted for something.

But when it came to giving a little boy a home, when it came to fulfilling the longing in her heart, or to answering her dream of a family, love wasn't enough.

Clay took one look at Holly's red eyes as she opened the door, and his greeting died on his lips. "Holly? Are you okay?"

She met his gaze with a blank stare, as if unsure why he was there or who he even was. "Clay, what are you…" She blinked away some of the distance from her eyes, and her shoulders slumped. "The movies. That's tonight, isn't it?"

Concern for Holly pushed aside any blow to his ego about forgetting their date. Her pale face and the hollow look in her eyes reminded him of his mother after his father's death. Days where she'd wandered the house in an impenetrable fugue, staving off grief and pain by refusing to feel anything. His heart suddenly pounding with worry, he demanded, "What's wrong?"

Shaking her head, she turned back into the apartment. "I have to go to the store."

The explanation was the last he'd expected and one that made no sense. "You want to go shopping?"

"No. I have to…return something." She spun in a circle, running a hand through her damp hair, but Clay couldn't be sure she saw anything. Her focus seemed directed inward, replaying some vision she seemed determined to escape. Movement was key as she caught her coat on one pass, slipping it on one arm before she grabbed her purse and hooked it over her coatless shoulder.

Like someone who had caught a sleepwalker during the darkness of her journey, Clay didn't know which would be worse—stopping her or letting her continue the frenzied motion. "Holly, what—"

"I have to take it back!" Her voice rose as she met his gaze for the first time. Pain filled her eyes, casting dark shadows. "I never should have bought it. It was a stupid thing to do, and now it's just sitting here. Useless and, and *empty.*"

The arm wearing the coat slapped to her right, and as Clay followed the movement and saw the package, he understood. Understood and felt a gut-deep denial that nearly dropped him to his knees.

No. It wasn't possible. Life couldn't be that cruel…that wrong.

A picture of a smiling child in a car seat covered the box.

His heart ached for her. "Holly, I am so sorry."

At his words her frantic movements gradually slowed and then stilled. Sucking in a deep breath, the first he thought she'd taken since he'd arrived, she whispered, "You know?"

Nodding, Clay confessed the smaller of his transgressions. "I overheard your conversation with Catherine Hopkins the other day."

"You know and you still… I thought…" Refuting whatever she'd thought with a shake of her head, she said, "It doesn't matter. You're still here, but it doesn't matter."

His jaw clenched at her words. He wanted it to matter, dammit. He wanted his presence to make a difference, to help. Ignoring the ache in his chest, Clay led Holly to the couch and settled beside her. "I'm still here," he echoed. "Right here." And he wasn't going anywhere, not as long as she needed… someone.

Her voice still held on to the emotionless monotone, but she sank against his side as she confessed, "I know all the reasons why I was turned down. I'm young. I'm single. I'm far from rich. But Lucas needs a mother."

Clay softly filled in the words she didn't say. "I know how much you love him."

Her gaze locked on the car-seat box, she said, "I told myself not to get my hopes up. But the car seat was on sale." Her voice broke. "I wanted so badly to believe this time things might work out."

Clay wrapped his arms around her again, feeling her delicate shoulders shake with the suppressed sobs she'd buried inside. The words *this time* revealed the depth of her sorrow. Not only was Holly mourning the loss of the child she wouldn't be allowed to raise, she was still battling her own memories of abandonment.

"Do you remember at Hopewell House when you asked me what Christmas present I never got as a kid?" Holly asked, tears still clogging her throat.

"I remember."

"I always wished for a family. A *real* family, not a temporary foster home." Her hand fluttered in a hopeless gesture. "Now, I'm twenty-four years old and still making wishes that don't come true."

The defeat in her voice worried Clay as much as her tears had. In an attempt to protect her heart from greater hurt, she refused to hope. "Holly, you can't give up."

"I did everything!" she protested. "I met with the caseworker. I had my apartment inspected. I took all the certification classes. It didn't matter. Now, with Hopewell House closing, I won't even see Lucas and the other kids anymore."

Sharp-edged guilt sliced through Clay as his association with Kevin Hendrix dragged him deeper and deeper. He had to find a way to reverse the damage he'd caused. There had to be something he could do....

"What if—"

"No, Clay." Holly shook her head as she pulled out of his embrace and brushed away her tears, along with her impossible dreams. She'd played that painful game too many times. She'd counted on what-ifs and maybes, stacking them one on top of the other like a house of cards. Each time they'd fallen, she'd built them up again; this last time, with hopes of fostering Lucas, she'd reached even higher and fallen harder than ever.

Never again, she swore. She wouldn't survive risking her heart that way again. "I can't do it. I can't try anymore."

Even as she said the words, the emptiness that had always surrounded her seemed to seep into her soul. The feeling haunted her. She wanted to run but couldn't escape the emptiness inside. How much worse would it be once Lucas was placed with another foster family and the group home closed?

"Holly, if I can do anything to fix this, I will."

Closing her eyes, she ignored his promise. Instead, she focused on the determination in his voice and the contrasting gentleness of his touch. She sank deeper into the sensual spell as he brushed his fingertips across her cheeks, her temple, her jaw.

Lifting eyelids that felt weighted, Holly met his gaze. Desire darkened his blue eyes, and the arms that cradled her so gently tightened.

Clay took a deep breath. "This isn't a good idea."

She'd sensed his protest before he'd even spoken, the battle he waged written in his dark frown and the shift of his body, breaking heated contact with hers. Ignoring the words, she remembered their earlier kisses. The play of skin against skin, tasting, teasing, all a prelude to greater intimacy. Her heart pounded, and she stroked his lower lip with her thumb. "Are you sure?"

"No. I mean, yes." He groaned deep in his throat and caught her hand. The battle for control had turned into a full-fledged war. Desire sharpened his features, and his breathing quickened. She found herself matching the rhythm, inhaling the scent of his cologne and wanting to take even more of him inside.

"I don't want you to regret this," he said.

"You think I will?"

Some unnamed emotion burned in his eyes. Nodding slowly, he forced the words out. "You might."

Then again, she might not. All Holly knew was that she refused to suffer through what-ifs and maybes anymore. She was done with dreams, done with imagining some perfect family in some perfect future. Clay was here, now, and the desire she felt was real.

He could take away the loneliness, the sense of loss that had plagued her for so long. In Clay's arms, she would be whole, if only for a while.

"I won't," she promised. And in case he worried that she might expect more than he could give, she added, "All I want is this." She brushed her lips against his jaw. "All I want is tonight."

"Holly." Her name ended on a groan. "You should have so much more."

"Shh." She mentally added *should haves* to the *what-ifs* and *maybes* standing between her and what she could definitely have.

She wanted Clay; nothing else mattered.

Her mouth reached his throat, and she parted her lips. His pulse thrummed against her tongue. With his chest pressed to her breasts, she felt his breath catch and his heart slam against his ribs. Arousal filled her head with an intoxicating giddiness, and she pulled his head down to meet her kiss.

Their lips met and clung. Longing stole her breath. Desire surged between them, heady and potent. The walls she'd erected long ago tumbled down.

Finding bare skin at the back of his neck, she relished the heat radiating from his body. She imagined his naked flesh pressed to hers, and her breasts tightened. Without giving herself time to think, she sought the hem of Clay's sweater. She ran her hands over his smooth, muscular back, eliciting another deep groan.

"Holly." He murmured her name against her lips as he pressed her back against the cushions, and they sank onto the couch without breaking the kiss. She didn't know how she could have forgotten how good pure, physical pleasure could feel. Or maybe nothing had ever felt this good before... The languid, drugging kisses left her weak. His tongue circled hers, pulling her deeper into the swirling desire.

Holly broke the kiss, and with his taste still on her lips, she tried to strip off his sweater. Clay was faster, though. Catching her wrists, he stretched out over her. "Holly, wait."

With her hands pinned to the armrest, she couldn't pull him back down, couldn't bare his skin to her touch. "Clay, please."

A sensual plea filled her voice, but an ironclad control locked his jaw. "I don't think—"

"Good. Don't think," she interrupted, entwining her legs

with his. Despite the layers of clothing separating them, their bodies rocked together in an erotic rhythm.

He closed his eyes to the promised pleasure, but not before Holly saw that flash of emotion pierce his blue eyes. Was it guilt? But that didn't make sense unless—

"Clay, don't you want me?" The desire dimmed, leaving her vulnerable, lost.

His eyes snapped open. "God, yes. You have to know that."

"Then...why?"

"I never meant... I'd never want to do anything to hurt you."

"You won't," she vowed. The only way she'd get hurt would be if she expected too much, if she opened her heart or tricked herself into believing this night could mean more than sex. "I want you, too."

"As simple as that?" The muscle in his jaw vibrated, and his eyebrows rose in doubt, questioning her word.

"We're consenting adults," she said, with a blasé sophistication she didn't truly feel. "Why make things complicated?"

After all, it was just sex. If she kept repeating that, surely she'd start to believe it. Holly thought she stood a chance of convincing herself...until she caught the determined glint in Clay's eyes.

"Why, indeed," he challenged, and Holly realized he was out to prove it meant more to him. To both of them.

She swallowed hard, feeling the first flicker of unease. "Clay."

He silenced her faint protest in a heated kiss that scorched her worries to cinders. No doubt those fears would rise again, like a phoenix from the ashes, but Holly couldn't think about that. She couldn't think beyond his kiss.

With one of Clay's hands holding both of hers against the armrest, Holly couldn't move. Not that she had any intention of resisting. But when he teased the buttons of her sweater open, his knuckles brushing her breasts, she would have shoved his hands aside and pulled the sweater over her head. But he refused to hurry, refused to simply take, refused to limit the passion between them to *just sex*.

Fear stirred to life, but then his long fingers reached the final button over her trembling stomach. He parted the material slowly, the anticipation building to desperation.

"Beautiful," he murmured, his deep, passion-filled voice sending a wave of goose bumps shivering across her exposed skin.

For the first time, Holly didn't worry about her breasts being big enough, her stomach flat enough, her entire body sexy enough. Clay thought she was beautiful, and that, she decided, was more than enough. Her hands flexed, then stilled. She was trapped, not so much by his tender grip, but by the consuming strength of her own passion.

Her heart raced and her breath stalled in her throat as his fingers inched up her stomach. With a flick of the clasp at the center of her bra, Clay released a floodgate of sensation. Heat pooled low in her belly, and she whispered his name. He pushed the lace-covered cups aside and claimed her breast, first with the stroke of his fingers, then with the indescribable pleasure of his mouth.

At the sweet, sharp tug of her nipple, her hips rose off the couch. Clay shifted his weight more firmly against her. The stroke of his tongue over her breast and the friction of his muscled thigh between her own built the heat inside from spark to flame to inferno.

Holly could hardly believe it. He hadn't even touched her below the waist, but—oh! Just the thought of those strong, masculine fingers sliding from her breast to her belly, to beneath the waistband of her slacks, to stroke that sensitive flesh between her thighs…

She cried out again, and Clay released her hands just in time for her to tunnel her fingers into his dark hair, clinging to him, as the pleasure burned out of control. With both hands now free, he gripped her hips, holding her trembling body tight to his.

Limp from the release, she sank back against the couch cushions, her hair fanning out over the armrest. Gradually, her breathing evened, her heartbeat slowed, and the tremors shaking her body eased to the occasional twinge, intent on re-minding her that the incredible foreplay was just a preview.

Clay pressed a tender kiss to her forehead, and Holly knew she'd eventually have to open her eyes. Even with them closed, she felt exposed. Vulnerable. Stripped defenseless by the emo-tional failure to adopt Lucas and the physical surrender to needs she rarely acknowledged. All without actually making love.

Clay was right. It wasn't just sex. Could she really hope to guard her heart once they took that even more intimate step?

His surprising chuckle eased her panic. "If you're trying to fool me into thinking you've fallen asleep, I'm not buying it."

"Nothing that immature. I'm going for the theory that if I don't open my eyes, you can't see me."

"Not working," he murmured, his voice deep and rich in her self-imposed darkness. The cushions shifted beneath her as he levered his body away from hers. "I see you."

His hands brushed her breasts, and Holly's eyes flew open at the click of her bra clasp. "Clay, what—"

By the time she had formed the half-asked question, he had already buttoned her sweater. He stretched out beside her, a tight fit on the couch, and pulled her into his arms.

Lifting her head, she stared at him. Refusing to be embar-rassed, she said, "But you didn't…"

Desire still burned in his eyes, tempered by a relentless control. "I know. That was just for you."

"Just for me, huh? I don't remember that gift from 'The Twelve Days of Christmas,'" she teased, until she recalled the song's phrasing. *My true love gave to me…*

No, she wouldn't think about love.

But as she rested her head on Clay's chest, listening to the steady drum of his heartbeat, thoughts of his generosity, his kindness, his understanding, his undeniable sexiness played out in her head. "Thank you," she murmured against the nubby texture of his sweater.

The low vibration of his laughter tickled. "It was my pleasure."

"Not for that!" Holly protested. "Well, yes, for that. But also for listening. For caring. For not telling me I was crazy to want to be Lucas's foster mother or that I'm better off because the foster adoption didn't go through."

Clay threaded his fingers through her hair, sifting the dark strands. "I would *never* say something so stupid. You can't give up, Holly," he urged.

"What am I supposed to do? Keep wishing on stars?"

He ran a finger down her soft cheek and smiled down at her. "No. All you have to do is believe in Santa Claus."

The knock on the door took Holly by surprise. She looked away from the television to glance at the clock. It was nearly ten. Although she hadn't felt up to going to the movies, she would have liked Clay to stay, but she'd been unable to ask and he'd left, with his promise ringing in her ears.

She'd tried numbing her mind with television, but sitting on the couch where they'd nearly made love, images of his kiss, his touch, played over the black-and-white movie on the screen. Hitting the off button on the remote, she went to answer the door. A six-foot-tall Christmas tree greeted her. "What on earth?"

Clay peeked out from behind the tree's pointed top. A touch out of breath, he grinned boyishly. "I've decided your lack of Christmas spirit is due to missing one of these."

The pine scent drifted toward her. An emotional ache clogged her throat as she reached out to a supple branch. "I can't believe you did this." Except she could. Every time she turned around, he was surprising her with touching, thoughtful gestures. "I don't even have any—"

"Decorations are in the hall," he grunted, maneuvering the tree through the narrow doorway.

Holly carried in the shopping bags and followed Clay to the living room. "Look at all this! Lights, bows, garland, glass balls."

"And an angel for the top. Everything you need for a tree." He adjusted the stand in the corner of the room and took a step back. "What do you think? Is it straight?" A lock of dark hair fell over her forehead, and pine needles stuck to his sweater.

A frightening rush of emotion swept through Holly. "It's wonderful."

And terrifying, she thought, knowing how close she was to completely falling for him.

His eyes darkened, and Holly wondered how much of that truth he could read in her face. "Guess we should start with the lights."

An hour later, they had trimmed a beautiful tree. In the past, Holly hadn't bothered. Decorating for the holidays seemed like too much work when she was the only one there to enjoy it. After all, she had told herself, Christmas was for children.

Reaching out, she straightened a bow. She'd missed celebrating. Every adult needed a moment or two of childlike wonder and a time to believe in miracles.

As Holly picked up the last of the shopping bags, she gave Clay a mock frown. "No mistletoe?"

"I, um, guess I forgot."

"That's okay," she said, taking a step closer. "We don't need to rely on old-fashioned traditions."

They might not need them, but Holly wanted them. She was as old-fashioned and traditional as they came. Her nothing-but-sex talk had obviously been a facade built to protect her heart, and Clay still didn't know what had goaded him to break through the fragile barrier and force her to admit the truth. Especially when he was the one hiding behind a lie.

But despite the guilt twisting his gut, Clay knew telling the truth wasn't the answer. If Holly knew he—and his *money*—backed Kevin Hendrix and Hopewell House's closing, she'd never forgive him. Never give him the chance to make up for the damage he'd caused.

But as Holly rose on tiptoe to brush her lips against his, Clay wasn't thinking about his deal with Kevin Hendrix. He wasn't thinking about Hopewell House. He wasn't thinking of anything beyond the soft, seductive pressure of Holly's kiss. The bedroom suddenly seemed too far away. They could lie by the tree and let the flashing lights paint their naked bodies….

"Don't tease me, Clay," Holly whispered, her lips moving against his as she spoke. "No starting something you won't finish. Not this time."

It had nearly killed him earlier to let her go after the way she'd come apart in his arms, but if the walk through the frigid tree lot hadn't cooled his raging body, the cold, hard slap of his conscience certainly had. He'd vowed to stay away from Holly until he found a way to undo the damage he'd caused, and he'd found an answer in her words.

I'm young…single. As her words played over and over in his head, an idea had formed. A simple idea…a brilliant idea.

Fighting back a groan, he broke the kiss. "Holly, wait." He pulled a gust of air into his oxygen-deprived lungs and rested his forehead against hers. "I want to ask you something." He stepped away and picked up the jacket he'd draped over the back of the couch. "What if there was a way for you to adopt Lucas?"

Hurt flashed in her eyes. "There isn't! I've already told you all the reasons why. I'm too young. I'm single. I'm—"

"What if you weren't?"

"What if I wasn't...what?"

Reaching into the jacket pocket, he pulled out a tiny black box. "What if," he began as he opened the box to reveal a platinum and diamond engagement ring, "you weren't single?"

Chapter Eight

With her blood beating in her ears, Holly was certain she'd heard wrong, but the diamond ring winking from the jeweler's box spoke louder than words. "You want to marry me?" Her knees gave out, and she would have sunk to the floor if the couch hadn't gotten in the way.

"I know it sounds a little crazy."

"A little?" she echoed, staring up at him. A sudden thought struck her. "Does this have *anything* to do with what happened earlier? Because I told you, I don't expect—"

"You don't expect much, do you, Holly?" He sat on the couch, beside her. "After the way you grew up, you don't even expect the everyday things most people take for granted. Things like home and family."

Compassion and a wealth of understanding shone in his eyes. How could a man who'd been born with all that money could buy see so clearly into her heart? "It hurts too much to hope," she whispered.

"No, sweetheart, it doesn't. Not when it's possible to make those hopes and dreams come true." Setting the ring box aside, he cupped her face in his hands, as if he could convince her with his touch. "I know how much you want to adopt Lucas. I know what a good mother you'd be. I can help you." Urgently, he whispered, "Let me help you."

"But we barely know each other! And you're not...*we're* not—"

"Not what, Holly?"

"Not in love," she finished on a whisper, wondering if her words were true. Oh, it would be so easy to fall for Clay. But she couldn't begin to believe a man as worldly, as sophisticated as Clay Forrester would ever love a nobody like her.

A frown shadowed his features, and Holly knew she had that much right. "I thought I loved my first wife, and Victoria certainly said she loved me. But if that was love..." He shook his head, dismissing even the thought of the emotion. "Well, it wasn't nearly enough to keep our marriage on track. After the divorce, I knew I'd never stake my future on such a 'here today, gone tomorrow' emotion again."

As he met her gaze, the shadows cleared, determination radiating from his blue eyes. "I want more than that. I want something...real. Something I can build a future on."

"And marrying me—" Holly heard the wonder in her own voice "—will give you the future you want?"

"I hope it'll give us the future *we* want. You, me and Lucas. After Victoria, I pretty much gave up on having a family. I threw myself into the business, totally focusing on myself and what I wanted, without thinking of anyone else."

Guilt twisted his expression, and Holly hated hearing the way he viewed himself. "Clay, that is not true! You are one of the least self-centered people I know!"

He opened his mouth to deny her praises, but she pressed on, more determined to convince him. "Look at all you've done for Hopewell House. Dressing up as Santa might not seem like a big deal, but trust me, those kids will never forget it. And what about the house you found for the Hopewell sisters?"

Listening to her own argument, Holly started to think she was crazy for not jumping at his proposal, even if the strings attached did keep his heart closed. Maybe he didn't love her, but he cared. He was selfless and giving, sexy enough to steal her breath, sweet enough to steal her heart.

"That was all you. I never would have done any of that if not for you." Some inscrutable emotion chased across his features, only to disappear into the determined planes and angles of his handsome face. "I'm not the man you think I am, but I want to be. Just think about it," he urged. "And think about this."

Clay kissed her again, channeling all his persuasion into that one kiss. His lips played against hers, stroking and parting. Heated memories filled her thoughts, and Holly relived the exquisite feel of his hands opening her sweater, exploring skin. But this time, his hands remained tensed on her shoulder blades as he let the kiss convey all the longing and desire pounding between them.

When Clay finally pulled back, he lifted her hand and wrapped her fingers around the tiny black box. "I'll call you tomorrow."

After locking the door behind him, Holly crossed the room on shaky legs and collapsed onto the couch. *Think about it… Think about this….* Like she could think of anything else! Her entire body felt overheated and restless. A cold shower would do some good, but she didn't move. Instead, she wrapped her arms around her waist, holding on to the feeling. She never felt so alive as she did in Clay's arms.

Oh, he didn't play fair! He'd told her he needed her. She'd waited her whole life to hear those words. Now Clay had breathed life into the dream she'd given up on. He was offering her everything she'd ever wanted.

Except his love. A tiny twinge in her heart protested.

Holly ignored the emotional ache. The proposal might not be the norm, but when had her life ever included what most people took for granted? Parents, siblings, a permanent home— she'd learned to live without any of those.

Eleanor Hopewell had said things happened for a reason. Maybe those hard-earned lessons had brought Holly to this decision. A decision where a practical marriage would make the dream of adopting Lucas a reality.

Maybe Clay was right. Maybe marriage wasn't as crazy as it sounded.

The lights on the Christmas tree winked, the bright colors reflected in the diamond solitaire resting in its box. The ring sat where she'd left it the night before, but thoughts of the ring—and more importantly—Clay's proposal had followed Holly all day.

After a mostly sleepless night, she'd gone about mundane chores in a fog. She'd vacuumed, done a load of laundry, gone grocery shopping, but the one errand she hadn't completed was the one she'd been so intent on the night before—returning the car seat. All because of the exquisite ring sitting on her secondhand, water-spotted coffee table.

She jumped when the phone rang, mocking the pretense that she hadn't been waiting for Clay's call. Her heart pounded as she picked up the receiver. "Hello?"

"Hi, Holly. It's Clay."

His deep voice was as seductive as a caress, and her gaze immediately locked on the engagement ring. Struggling to maintain her calm, she barely managed a greeting. "Hi."

Clay didn't have the same problem. His words were calm and clear as he asked, "Have you been thinking about my proposal?"

Holly might have suspected he could read her mind, except she'd thought of nothing else since he'd left. Was the same question spinning through his head?

That was hard to believe, but then everything about his proposal seemed too good to be true. He was offering her the chance to be Lucas's foster mother; all she had to do was say yes.

Say yes…say yes…say yes. The words echoed in the pulse of her veins, the rhythm of her breathing.

"I… Yes, I've been thinking about it."

A pause followed her words, as if he was waiting for an answer. When she didn't say anything, he murmured, "I don't want to pressure you."

"You aren't." But the pressure was there, building hour by hour as the Hopewell House closing drew nearer.

"Then is it all right if I come in?"

"Come in? Where are you?"

"Right outside."

Holly stared at the closed door, one that she'd believed had slammed shut on her chance to be Lucas's mother the day before, but now… Now, it wasn't just Clay standing on the other side. It was her whole future, a bright, wonderful future she'd never imagined. All she had to do was turn the knob, throw open the door, and take the biggest step she'd ever taken in her life.

The question was, did she dare?

"I'll be right there."

Opening the door and just seeing him, his dark hair and broad shoulders dusted with melting snow, his easygoing smile betrayed by the intensity burning in his blue eyes, sent joy rushing through her at a speed that nearly lifted her off her feet and propelled her straight into his arms.

Instead, she stepped back to let him inside. He shrugged out of his jacket and passed it to her waiting hands. The scent of damp leather and masculine cologne drifted from the material, and Holly fought the urge to bury her nose in the collar. Instead, she draped the jacket over the back of a chair. The leather was cold from the frigid Chicago night, but the lining still warm from the heat of his body.

"So," Clay said as he stepped behind her, close enough for his breath to tease the hair tucked behind her ear.

Her hand fisted around his jacket. Frozen on the outside, burning up inside. That exactly described how she felt at the moment, and she swallowed hard against a suddenly dry throat. "So," she echoed weakly.

"It's been twenty-four hours," he said. "Have you thought about it? Am I crazy?"

Holly nearly collapsed over the chair once she realized Clay wasn't asking point-blank for an answer to his proposal. "Certifiable," she told him, with a shaky laugh, turning to face him on trembling legs. "But you know what they say. Takes one to know one."

His eyes darkened, and she knew he hadn't missed the underlying meaning. If he was crazy enough to ask her to marry him, well, she was crazy enough to consider it.

But crazy or not, she wasn't ready to answer. Not yet. So when Clay started to speak, she said, "Tell me more about your first marriage."

He blinked in surprise at the sudden request. "What do you want to know?"

"I, um…" Although she felt as though she was prying, as the woman Clay had proposed to, Holly had a right to know. She walked into the living room and headed for the couch, only to recall what had happened the last time they sat there. Just remembering was enough to give the run-down piece of furniture a satin-and-lace aura. Veering around the suddenly seductive sofa, Holly led the way to the kitchen and settled onto one of the chairs. "What was she like?"

Hesitating, Clay joined her at the small tile-topped table,

considering the question rather than spitting out the first insult that came to mind. "You know the expression 'life of the party'? Well, Victoria took it one step further than that." He gave a short laugh. "She *was* the party. She was beautiful, fun, outgoing. Outrageous."

Holly tried not to think about how different she was from the woman he'd described. Like Clay, Victoria lived a life of champagne and caviar, and even though he'd asked Holly to marry him, Holly couldn't forget she was apple juice and tuna fish.

"Everyone said we made the perfect couple," Clay added.

Jealousy and insecurity squirmed inside her, reminding Holly that no one would ever see her as the perfect match for a man like Clay Forrester, but she squashed the nasty emotions. After all, truly perfect couples didn't get divorced.

"So what happened?" she asked.

"When we got married, I expected to settle down. Victoria took a different approach. Maybe she was afraid of losing her identity as part of a married couple, but she started going out even more."

"And then your father died."

Clay nodded. "I had to work longer hours." He ran his thumbnail along a joint in the table, lost in the past. "I wanted the marriage to work, I did. But nothing helped. It wasn't enough. *I* wasn't enough."

Old pain scraped his words. Reaching out, Holly covered his hand with hers. She wouldn't have thought they'd have such a thing in common, but she certainly understood the sense of failure that came from admitting her best simply wasn't good enough. "I know how that feels."

Clay turned his hand, linking their fingers, and she stared at their joined hands, a physical bond mirroring the emotional connection.

"When I couldn't give Victoria the time and attention she needed, well, she found someone who could."

Holly sucked in a startled breath. "Oh, Clay. I am so sorry, but what your ex did had *nothing* to do with you! There was something lacking in *her* if she thought she had to look for attention outside of your marriage."

How could his ex-wife have been so foolish to think she could find a man better than Clay? He was wonderful, everything a woman could hope for.

So what else are you hoping for? She asked herself. That she, of all people, might hold out for more than Clay had offered struck Holly into silence. Maybe it wasn't everything she'd dreamed of, but in some ways, it was much more. Because never in her wildest dreams had she imagined Clay Forrester proposing or offering to help her adopt Lucas. It was as close to a Christmas miracle as she'd ever see. Was she really expecting more?

"No," she said, the word nearly bursting from her lips.

Suddenly looking edgy, Clay asked, "No, what?"

"No. I mean, yes!"

"Okay, you've lost me."

"Yes, I'll marry you."

He froze. "You mean it?"

Holly gave a shaky laugh. "As long as you still do. If you've changed your mind, forget I said anything."

"I haven't changed my mind. I just—" Pushing away from the table, he patted down his pockets. "The ring. Where's the ring?"

She waved a hand toward the living room. "The coffee table."

His long strides carrying him into the other room, Clay grabbed the black velvet box. Holly couldn't begin to decipher the emotions flickering across his features as he turned back toward her. A tremor of worry shook her at his somber expression. "This is going to work, Holly. You'll see. I'm going to do everything I can to make you happy."

Pushing aside her own worries to reassure him, Holly insisted, "You already have."

He swallowed hard and said, "Let's do this right," as he dropped to one knee before her.

"Wait! Clay, I already said yes!"

"I know." His earlier tension eased. "Which is going to make asking much easier this time. Holly Bainbridge, will you marry me?"

Blinking back tears, she nodded. "Yes."

He slid the ring onto her finger, then lifted her hand to his lips. The tenderness in his gaze nearly held her spellbound. It was a moment when she might have expected words of love, but she shoved the thought aside.

Just as well, because when Clay did speak, the words were pragmatic. "Should we set a date?"

She hesitated briefly, then pushed on. "I'd like it to be as soon as possible."

Silently, she vowed not to expect too much from Clay or their marriage. Unlike his first marriage, he'd never have to worry that she would ask for more than he could give.

"I think we'll have a better chance of getting Lucas if we apply before he's placed with a new foster family," she added.

"Right." He stood suddenly and shoved his hands, along with the empty ring box, into his pockets. "There's just one thing we need to do."

"Just one thing?" Holly asked, feeling excitement and a serious case of nerves going a few rounds in her stomach. "I can think of a hundred."

"You're probably right about that. But first, we need to tell my family."

"Oh, of course," she said weakly.

Family. The very word took her back to the past, where her hopes and dreams of finding a family of her own had ended in heartbreak. And her excitement took a serious hit as she realized that this wasn't about being good enough anymore: it was about being good enough for Clay.

Chapter Nine

After lighting the final candle, Holly surveyed the table and the five place settings. Clay had arranged the family gathering at his penthouse to announce their engagement. She wrapped her arms around her waist, trying to still the butterflies in her stomach. What would his family think of their sudden plans? What would they think of *her?*

Clay embraced her from behind. "The table looks great, and the food smells wonderful."

"It should," she said. "The caterers did a great job."

"Hey." He jiggled his arms slightly. "You aren't still nervous, are you?"

More like terrified. Clay was the only son, the golden boy who took over the business after his father died. His family adored him. Certainly they expected only the best for him. How was she supposed to pass muster?

She'd splurged on new clothes, wanting to make a good impression. The soft lilac sweater and matching calf-length skirt had a touch of silver embroidery at the hem, on the sleeves, and along the glass buttons. Holly had thought the outfit elegant…until she stepped inside Clay's penthouse for the first time and saw what true elegance was.

The high-ceilinged foyer opened into the living room, where a wall-sized flat-screen television held court amid original works of art. The polished hardwood floors added warmth to the masculine, earth-tone furnishings, including two camel-colored leather couches and an antique trunk coffee table.

The kitchen was a gourmet chef's dream, with state-of-the-art appliances, black granite counters, and glass-front cherry cabinets. Holly felt like a fraud for using one of the double ovens to keep the catered food warm.

Clay had given her the caterer's number, and when she'd mentioned his name, Holly had practically heard the man on the other end of the line snap to attention. Kristoff's was one of the city's premiere restaurants, nearly impossible to get into, from what she'd heard, and yet they'd bent over backward to take on the last-minute catering job.

The food promised to be divine, but she worried the professionally prepared dishes branded her a fake. Eliza Doolittle at the ball, *Pretty Woman* at the opera. Holly was no Audrey Hepburn, no Julia Roberts. And she wasn't sure she could pull this off.

Turning in Clay's arms, she asked almost desperately, "Are you sure we shouldn't tell your family the truth?"

"The truth?"

"You know, about why we're getting married."

Clay dropped his arms to his sides and stepped back. "No."

"But wouldn't it be so much easier for them to understand?" she pleaded. "Instead of expecting them to believe this is some whirlwind love match?"

He studied her quietly for a moment, his normally open expression unreadable. "This is our marriage, Holly, and it's our business. Don't get me wrong. I love my family. But this is our decision, not theirs."

Determination straightened his stance, making his shoulders seem broader and stronger than ever. She'd seen him like this before. When he'd faced off against Albert Jensen at the company party and again when he'd knocked down her fears and protests about marrying him.

Holly loved his fierce sense of right and wrong and his conviction to stand up against those who opposed him. But she couldn't quell the fear that their marriage would put his family on the opposite side.

Slipping back into his more typical optimism, he said, "Don't worry. Everything will be fine." Before he had the chance to continue, the doorbell rang. He glanced at his watch. "That'll be my mother. My sister is always late."

"Well, dinner was great."

Holly smiled down the table at Clay's brother-in-law, Dan Cunningham. A former football player turned sportscaster, the blond man had the widest shoulders and biggest smile she'd ever seen. He'd accepted her readily enough, but she attributed that acceptance to the food she'd dished out. When Clay had first told her what to order, she'd feared they'd have leftover London broil for weeks. But by the time Dan had taken thirds, she'd started to worry the food might run out.

"Yes, Holly, the food was wonderful," Anne seconded.

Holly offered a hesitant smile to Clay's sister, but the expression quickly slipped away as Jillian Forrester asked, "I do believe it's Kristoff's, isn't it?"

Though well into her fifties, Clay's mother had a style and beauty any woman would envy. Her blond hair was meticulously swept into a French twist, emphasizing the classic bone structure, which age would never touch. Her beige silk suit undoubtedly boasted a designer label Holly had never heard of and a price tag she couldn't imagine. Simple, yet expensive statements in gold glittered at the woman's ears, throat, wrist and finger.

"Yes, Kristoff's did cater the dinner." Holly tried to tell herself that she hadn't heard the disapproval ringing in Jillian's voice, but it was the simple touch of Clay's hand around hers that filled her with confidence. Smiling at his mother, she said, "You must be very familiar with them to recognize their food."

A sudden fit of coughing overcame Anne. She reached for her napkin, hiding behind the linen cloth. Her husband tapped her between the shoulder blades, but Anne waved aside his concern. "I'm fine." She seemed to seek out Clay's gaze. "Sorry," she said, with a smile.

"Is everyone ready for dessert?" Holly asked.

"Did that come from Kristoff's as well?" Jillian questioned.

"No," Clay answered. "Holly made it herself. It's a chocolate cake."

Holly held her breath, waiting for Jillian to say she was allergic to chocolate. When the woman stayed silent, she pushed away from the table.

Clay stood and took her hand again. "Before we serve dessert, Holly and I have an announcement to make." He lifted her left hand and kissed her cold fingers. "I want you all to know that I've asked Holly to marry me."

A shocked gasp, the clatter of dropped silverware, then a heavy, tense silence filled the room. A silence so profound, Holly swore she could hear the rush of holiday traffic on the street below. Or maybe the sound was the blood rushing from her head.

As a child standing before prospective parents, the fear of rejection had been heartbreaking, but this was much, much worse. This time, rejection wouldn't just crush her; it would hurt Clay.

Finally, Dan broke the impasse, clapping Clay on the back and shaking his hand. Anne rounded the table and gave Holly a slight hug.

"Congratulations, Holly. Clay told me he'd met someone special, but I didn't expect him to move so quickly."

"I know it's sudden," Holly admitted. Her heartbeat slowed to a pace less than a hundred miles per hour, but she still felt shaky and wished for the security of Clay's hand in hers. Especially when she noticed his mother standing apart from the celebration.

"Have you set a date yet?" Anne asked.

"Christmas Eve," Clay said.

"But—but that's next week," Jillian gasped as she sank back into the dining-room chair.

Anne stared at her brother, her troubled gaze searching his. "Why so soon?"

Clay shrugged and placed his hands on Holly's shoulders. "Why wait?"

"There's no time to plan a wedding," his sister argued. "Holly, what does your family think about this?"

Anne seemed to expect her to add her own protest, but Holly said, "I don't have any family."

"So we've decided to get married by a justice of the peace," Clay added.

Jillian looked ready to faint. Even Anne shook her head. "Oh, Clay! What about all the things that make a wedding special? Like bridal showers?"

"Don't forget the bachelor party!" Dan chimed in, with a laugh.

"And what about a reception?" Anne continued.

Holly thought of being surrounded by hundreds of people she didn't know at a high-society reception and felt a wave of panic grip her stomach. She glanced back at Clay, her gaze pleading with him.

"We don't want any of those things," Clay said.

Holly breathed a sigh of relief, but the breath caught in her throat as she noticed Jillian watching them, disapproval stamped on her features.

* * *

Clay was stacking the dishes in the sink when he heard the door open, and turned to see his mother carrying in the dessert plates. "Mother, you're our guest. You don't have to clear the table."

Setting the dishes on the granite counter, she said, "I wanted a minute alone to talk to you."

Clay wasn't surprised. He'd known his announcement would come as a shock, but in the cold silence that had followed, he'd realized he'd made a mistake. He should have told his family earlier, preparing them and protecting Holly.

She looked so beautiful in the soft sweater outfit, which whispered over her feminine curves. She'd added some curls to her chestnut, shoulder-length hair, going out of the way to make a good impression, but not even the added makeup highlighting her eyes and cheeks had hidden her terror.

Looking at her, it had been heartbreakingly easy to picture her as a child, longing for a couple to give her a chance, only to face yet another rejection.

"I did this all wrong," he muttered.

"Well, it's not too late. You can take your time. There's nothing wrong with a nice long engagement," his mother reassured him.

"What I meant," he told her dryly, "is that Holly and I should have eloped. I never should have put her through this."

"Put her through this?" Jillian echoed. "You make it sound as though dinner with your family was pure torture for the poor girl."

Knowing Holly's insecurities, Clay muttered, "I don't doubt it."

Hearing the anger in his voice, his mother loosened her stubborn stance slightly. "I'm worried about you, Clay." Sorrow turned her mouth down at the corners, emphasizing the tiny lines that had appeared in the months since his father's death.

"I know, Mother." His irritation waned in response to her

obvious concern. "But you don't have to be. Holly's a wonderful woman. You just have to get to know her."

"Well," she said, raising an elegant eyebrow, "it's not like you've given us the chance."

The reproach brought a flush to Clay's face. He could have introduced Holly to his family without dropping the bomb that they were getting married.

Or he could have done as Holly had suggested and explained the real reason for the marriage. Not that Holly knew the whole truth behind the *real* reason, his conscience nagged. At least not about his relationship with Kevin Hendrix or the fact that he'd funded the project that was causing Hopewell House closing.

As much as Clay hated deceiving Holly, telling the truth at this point would do no good. It wouldn't help the Hopewell children; it wouldn't help Holly and Lucas become a family.

But he *could* help. Even though it meant lying to Holly to do it.

His mother placed her hand on his arm. "If you're going to do this, please have the wedding at the house. The ceremony doesn't have to be big or fancy, but at least your family will be there."

One look into her pleading eyes, and Clay felt himself weakening. Still, he said, "We'll see."

When she reached up to kiss his cheek, her familiar perfume, the brand his father had bought for her every year on Mother's Day, swept over Clay, along with dozens of memories. "I want you to be happy," she told him.

"We will be." Clay knew it. Just like he knew what Holly wanted and how hard she'd tried to make that dream come true. He didn't have to play guessing games to know what might or might not make her happy. She wanted to foster Lucas and give the little boy a home and family.

Once he and Holly married, once they adopted Lucas, Holly

would have the family she'd always wanted, and he would have… He would have Holly. He'd never wanted a woman the way he wanted her. In his bed, in his life.

"That's all I want," Jillian insisted, though the doubt written on her face told him she questioned if Holly was the woman for the job. "If anyone deserves a second chance at love, it's you."

Love.

Clay mentally shook his head, denying the possibility. This was a second chance, and this time he was going to do it right. He wasn't going to trust an insubstantial emotion like love. He cared about Holly, admired her, and he knew they had amazing chemistry. But they'd both been burned before, and as clear as Holly had been about what she wanted, Clay had been equally clear about what he was offering, and love was not on the table.

Clay watched the caseworker make notes on the clipboard she carried as Holly led the way down the hall. "We'll be converting the study into a bedroom for Lucas," she said, opening the door to let Cathcrine Hopkins see inside.

Reaching out, he entwined his fingers with Holly's and gave her trembling hand an encouraging squeeze. He wished he could instill his confidence in her. They *had* to be approved. He refused to think otherwise.

But the worry in Holly's eyes never went away. Neither did the fear of facing another rejection. He was doing everything in his power to see that this time things would be different.

The agency already had Holly's paperwork; Clay had pushed to get his own background check, interviews and home inspection done as quickly as possible. Fortunately, Holly's work with the Hopewells and her association with Lucas's caseworker had helped cut through the red tape. And with Hopewell House closing, the agency was trying to find replacement homes as quickly as possible.

Catherine consulted her clipboard. "When we talked before," she said to Holly, "you mentioned that you would have to leave Lucas at day care while you were at work."

"But that's not the case anymore. Once we marry, Holly can stay home with Lucas," Clay said, certain he was helping their case. Catherine made another note, her face impassive, but he could see the suspicion in her eyes. The caseworker had to wonder about the timing and haste of their marriage, but Clay had made sure to double and triple check every form. He didn't want to give Catherine any other reason to question the adoption.

"Thank you for your time, Mr. Forrester, Holly," Catherine said at the end of the inspection. Shaking their hands, she added, "The agency will be in touch."

Closing the door behind the woman, Clay turned to Holly, who leaned against the wall, as if all her strength had left along with the caseworker. "So, did we pass?" He intended the words to lighten the mood, but Holly stayed silent. "Okay, what's wrong? Something about the interview?"

"No, the interview went well. It's just… We never talked about me quitting work."

He blinked in surprise. "Isn't the whole reason for fostering Lucas that *you* can take care of him, not some stranger?"

"Well, yes."

Indecision still tugged at her eyebrows, and Clay forged on, determined to prove his point. "If you keep your job, how much time will you spend with him? You'll have breakfast in the morning and maybe an hour or two after dinner each night. Your days off will be the only quality time you'll have together."

"Single parents manage it."

Single parents. Was that how Holly thought of herself? Clay thought, with a wrenching twist in his gut. As a woman who wanted to raise a child *alone?*

"Sure, plenty of parents work full time if they *have* to. But you don't have to. I'm here for you. And for Lucas," he said, reminding himself of the reason why she had agreed to marry him.

He'd known he was taking a giant risk with his proposal, a huge step so early in their relationship, but once Holly had said yes, he'd thought it would bring them closer. Instead, their relationship had stalled.

"I know that, Clay. I do. But, well, I guess I'm not used to depending on anybody else. And it's just so hard waiting and not knowing." She gave a short laugh. "You'd think I'd be used to it after the last time."

When she'd been turned down.

Seeing the lingering hurt in her eyes, Clay's frustration waned. "It's all going to work out, Holly. You'll see. How are the wedding plans going?"

"Everything is completely under…your mother's control," Holly said wryly.

"If she gets to be too much—"

"No, I don't blame her for wanting the wedding at her home. You're her only son. She's just very…" Holly paused, and Clay sensed that she was searching for a polite word. "Purposeful."

"I guess since she didn't have a say in our relationship, she's going to put her mark on the wedding."

"She's arranged the food and the music. I'm wearing Anne's wedding dress, since the two of us are about the same size, and she'll be my bridesmaid. The only time I put my foot down was when your mother planned to use a different florist. I want Floral Fascinations to make the bouquets."

A stubborn light glowed in Holly's eyes, and Clay hid a smile. Holly could handle his mother. She was tougher than he gave her credit for. She'd had to be to weather all the disappointment in her life. His smile slowly faded. Was he setting her up for another one? If the adoption didn't go through—

Clay refused to consider the possibility. Holly would make

an amazing mother. Anyone could see that. After the way the system had failed her as a child, she deserved this shot at happiness. She deserved the chance to give Lucas the happy childhood fate had denied her and the family she'd always longed for. She deserved…

A husband who loves her, his conscience interjected. *One who is honest with her.*

"Clay, are you okay?" Holly's gentle voice and worried expression broke through the guilt surrounding him, and Clay cupped her face in his palms.

"I want you to be happy, Holly. No matter what happens, remember that."

"I am happy, Clay. I am," she insisted, and he might have believed her if the determined repetition hadn't sounded like she was trying to convince herself.

Taping up the final box, Holly surveyed her living room. She'd packed all her meager belongings, ready to move in with Clay. Pretty sorry testament to her personal life that the place still looked the same.

She'd never really bothered to decorate any of the many places she'd lived since she'd turned eighteen. None of them had felt like home.

Sinking onto the couch, she thought of Clay's penthouse. Would living there ever feel like home? He'd offered to hire a decorator, but what would be the point? His home was already furnished in such wonderfully masculine, neutral colors. They would have to convert a room for Lucas, of course, but Holly wanted to wait for the approval to adopt Lucas to go through. Until then, she didn't want to make any changes.

Didn't want to make changes. Her shaky laughter filled the room. She was quitting her job, giving up her apartment… *getting married!*

What bigger changes could she make?

Oh, were they doing the right thing? Could the love of a child make a marriage? Lucas's dimpled smile flashed in her mind, the memory as warm and joyful as holding the little boy in her arms. Lucas wasn't just any child. He was special. He'd crawled into her heart the first time she saw him. Wasn't it possible Lucas had had that same effect on Clay?

The ring of her cell phone took her by surprise. The phone was a gift from Clay, and she was still getting used to it.

Grabbing her purse off the kitchen counter, she fished out the small flip phone. "Hello?"

"Holly, it's Clay." Frustration filled his voice as he added, "This meeting with John Westfell is taking forever."

He'd promised to leave work early to help her pack. She quickly said, "Don't worry about it. I know how important it is."

And while she might not have known the whole story of Clay's first marriage, Holly had figured out his ex had resented his time at the office. She'd taken his words about Victoria's neediness and jealousy to heart and vowed not to make the same mistakes.

"Besides, I've got everything boxed up and ready to go," she added.

Silence filled the line. "Already? Holly, I told you I'd help."

"I know, but it was no big deal. A one-person job. Really," she insisted, feeling a touch defensive without knowing why. After all, she had moving down to an art form, so much so that she'd lost track of how many times she'd picked up and left. Hoping to lighten the moment, she teased, "You've seen my closet, remember? I don't have that many clothes."

"I remember." A smile entered his voice. "We're going to have to do something about that."

As she mentally compared her own off-the-rack sense of style with his mother's and sister's couture taste, discomfort flitted through her stomach. With a quick change of subject, she said, "I can take the boxes to your place, and the apartment manager is going to arrange for Goodwill to pick up the things I don't need. Of course, the furniture all stays. Although I was tempted to bring the couch with me," she added, her voice dropping to a seductive murmur she barely recognized. "I have some wonderful memories of that couch."

Stunned silence filled the line until Clay cleared his throat. "Yeah, well, I've got two couches at my place."

"I know." Feeling a touch of power at leaving him momentarily speechless, she added, "Leather, aren't they?"

"Uh-huh. Extra long."

A shiver raced through Holly at the sexy teasing. Whatever memories she had of her apartment or her past were nothing compared to the promise of life with Clay.

Chapter Ten

"The dress fits so well, no one will know it wasn't made for you," Anne told Holly.

The guest bedroom at Jillian Forrester's house had been turned into a makeshift bridal dressing room. Holly had hoped for some time alone, but once she slipped on the wedding gown, she discovered she couldn't dress herself.

Anne had come to her rescue, and her soothing voice calmed Holly's nerves. "All done." Anne took a step back. "Wow. Don't you look beautiful?"

Holly couldn't tear her gaze away from the mirror. Foregoing a veil, she wore her dark hair piled on top of her head, crowned with a sprig of baby's breath. The upswept style complemented the off-the-shoulder, long-sleeved dress. Seed pearls decorated the fitted bodice and formed a floral pattern on the full skirt. Anne had done her makeup, and Holly barely recognized the elegant woman staring back at her. But the wide, uncertain eyes, highlighted by mascara and eye shadow, were undeniably her own.

"It's a stunning dress, Anne." More beautiful than she could have imagined and definitely more than she could ever afford. Clay had wanted her to buy a gown of her own, but Holly had refused. Certainly he could afford it, but she didn't want him to think she was anything like his ex in her unending quest for more. "Thank you for letting me borrow it."

"I loved the dress the moment I saw it, and it's worth wearing more than once. I can only hope that you and Clay will be as happy as Dan and I have been."

The sentiment, combined with Anne's acceptance of the sudden marriage, sent tears rushing to Holly's eyes.

"Hey! Enough of that!" Anne warned. She handed Holly a tissue. "No bride wants to end up looking like a raccoon in her wedding photos."

Holly wiped her eyes and managed to calm her riotous emotions. The door opened after a brief knock, and Marilyn, her former coworker, stuck her head inside the doorway. "I have bouquets!" She passed the flowers to Holly and Anne.

The bouquets were stunning spirals of rosebuds that paled from a bright fuchsia to the lightest cream. Holly ran her fingers over the pink ribbon, which matched Anne's brides-maid dress.

"Everything's ready when you are," Marilyn announced.

Anne gave Holly a quick hug. "See you downstairs, sis."

The two women left, and Holly took as deep a breath as she could in the stay-lined bodice. Music floated through the open door, compliments of the string quartet Jillian Forrester had hired.

Sis. Anne had used the nickname to bolster Holly's confidence, but the word only added to her fears. The roses in the bouquet trembled. She'd never been a sister before. Or a wife. Or a mother.

It was what Holly had always wanted, but she'd never considered the pressure. Her life had been lonely, but not nearly as frightening. What if she couldn't be the mother Lucas needed or the wife Clay wanted?

The quartet began again, this time playing the wedding march, her cue to go downstairs, where everyone was waiting. Where the man she loved was waiting.

Her heart seized. Holly met her own shocked gaze in the mirror and knew it was true. She was about to marry the man she loved. The emotion wouldn't have seemed out of place for a normal bride, but she and Clay weren't going to have a normal marriage.

She'd said yes to his proposal and the limitations that went with it. He *cared* for her but wanted a marriage free of the emotional complications of love. She had to remember that and not be so foolish as to want more than Clay could give. She wouldn't do that to him.

Or to herself.

At the bottom of the stairs, Holly was aware of all the eyes focused on her. Although the invitations had been limited to friends and family, two dozen guests rose as Holly walked down the aisle. When she saw Clay, though, everyone else disappeared.

He stood with the minister in the bay-window alcove. Wearing a tuxedo, Clay looked so tall, so gorgeous, so *stunned*. He blinked, almost as though someone had thrown a light switch and his eyes needed to adjust. His throat moved as he swallowed, and his lips parted on a deep breath.

Holly ignored the ache in her heart, certain she was projecting her own nerves onto Clay. Still, she placed one foot in front of the other, each step carrying her closer to her new life.

From the corner of her eye, she caught sight of Lucas. Seated in Eleanor Hopewell's lap, on the aisle, he wore a miniature tuxedo, though his bow tie was off center and a cowlick tufted his blond curls. He waved exuberantly as she walked by.

Happiness bubbled inside her, nearly lifting her feet off the rose-petal-strewn runner. The overwhelming feeling erased her earlier nervousness. The chance to have Lucas in her life, to be his mother, was a gift, one Clay had given her. She would embrace the opportunity and not ask for anything more.

Catching sight of the gleam in Clay's blue eyes—like a cloudless sky on a spring day—she vowed that it would be more than enough. Over her pounding heartbeat, she heard the minister's words and Clay's response. She must have answered at the appropriate time, because the next thing Holly knew, Anne took the bridal bouquet, and Clay slipped the ring onto her finger. Her hands trembled, but she managed to slide the thin gold band onto his ring finger.

"I now pronounce you husband and wife."

That fire in Clay's eyes burned brighter as he bent his head. Holly rose on tiptoe to meet his tender kiss, a whisper-soft promise of things to come that made her heart beat faster and weakened her knees.

After the all-too-brief touch, family and friends separated the bride and groom. Anne gave Holly a hug, and she struggled to keep her balance as Lucas launched himself at her legs. Laughing, she picked up the little boy.

Lucas reached up and pointed at the baby's breath in her hair. "You look pretty, Miss Holly."

"Yes, she does, Lucas."

Holly turned to Eleanor and gave the woman a one-armed hug. "Thank you so much for coming and bringing Lucas."

The older woman's eyes brightened with tears. "I wouldn't have missed it. Lucas will be a part of your family soon. It's only right that he be here, too."

Her family! Hope beat a chaotic rhythm in her heart, and she hugged Lucas tightly. "Oh, Eleanor, I hope you're right."

"Of course, I am. Good things come in threes, you know."

A puzzled frown tugged at Holly's eyebrows. She knew her marriage and Lucas's adoption were certainly on that list, and she asked, "What's the third thing?"

"An anonymous donation was made for the Hopewell House children. A fund has been set up for each child."

"Anonymously?" Holly echoed, seeking out Clay. She spotted him posing for a casual picture in the alcove with his brother-in-law, and she knew. The donation might have been anonymous, but Clay couldn't hide the goodness in his heart. He was such a wonderful man. So kind, so generous…so easy to love.

"Isn't that incredible?" Eleanor asked.

"He is," Holly murmured.

"What was that, dear?"

"I mean, it is. Incredible," she agreed, seeing by the laughter sparkling in the other woman's eyes that she hadn't fooled her for a minute.

Glancing back at Clay, she caught his gaze, and his expression turned hungry. Sensual promise lit his eyes. Even from across the room, the look stole her breath.

"Excuse me, Holly," Anne said. "Mother wants to get the wedding party together for pictures."

Still tingling with awareness from Clay's heated gaze, Holly hoped she didn't look as flustered and breathless as she felt. Excusing themselves, Holly and Anne made their way across the room amid hugs and well wishes from friends.

Although her new sister-in-law's expression remained serious, laughter filled her voice as she said, "Don't worry. It only *seems* like these things last forever."

If Holly was impatient, she wasn't the only one. As the photographer arranged them in what felt like stiff, unnatural poses, Clay leaned close and whispered, "Soon."

The word sent a shiver racing through her. As the photographer turned them toward each other, Clay's arms slid around her waist, and she smoothed her hands across his muscular chest. The heat of his embrace seeped through to her skin despite the heavy satin.

His lips were mere inches away, and Holly imagined leaning forward to rediscover the taste and texture of his mouth. Anticipation thrummed in her veins, heating her blood, and *soon* couldn't come quickly enough.

The bright flash caught Holly off guard. She blinked, feeling like she'd awakened from a dream. Only the passion Clay felt, the promises he'd made, were real. And they were better, she insisted, than any dream of love she could imagine.

"Thank you, Mother. Everything was perfect." Even as Clay spoke, he sought out Holly. She was kneeling down to talk to Lucas, her full skirt flowing around her. He wondered if it would ruin the entire reception if he picked her up and carried her off without saying goodbye. He turned to find his mother watching him closely and figured she'd never forgive him.

"You're welcome, dear. Thank *you* for letting me be part of it."

"We couldn't have done it without you." He brushed a kiss across his mother's cheek just as Holly walked over and linked her arm through his.

Having overheard his comment, she added, "I'm amazed at the wonderful job you did, Mrs. Forrester."

Clay could almost feel Holly holding her breath, holding in her vulnerability as she waited for Jillian's reply. Mentally willing his mother to accept the compliment, to accept Holly, he reached over and squeezed the hand she'd placed on his arm.

He breathed a sigh of relief as his mother unbent slightly. "Well, I do have some experience with weddings."

"I can only imagine how elegant Anne's wedding must have been, considering what you accomplished in a matter of days.

The music, the decorations. And the cake!" Although Holly spoke to his mother, Clay caught the glance she aimed in his direction as she added, "The chocolate cake and strawberry filling were absolutely mouthwatering."

Despite her innocent expression, Clay caught the subtle, arousing reminder. He could still taste the strawberries, along with the sweetness of her kiss. Thanks to the cheesecake on the night they'd met as well as their wedding cake, Clay knew the flavor of strawberries would always remind him of Holly.

He could only imagine, now that they were married, how many other everyday tastes and textures would be forever linked to thoughts of her. How she would haunt his senses, becoming so much a part of him that he wouldn't be able to live without her—

"Clay?"

Holly's puzzled voice broke into his thoughts, and he gave a quick shake of his head. "Sorry, what were you saying?"

"Your mother offered to take the top layer of our cake home with her," she explained.

Clay didn't know that much about wedding traditions, but he was familiar with this one. The cake would be frozen and saved for their first anniversary. An entire year from now. Just that simple acknowledgment of their future eased some of the pressure crushing his chest.

"Ah yes, the cake," Jillian said. Then she surprised them both by confiding, "It was from Kristoff's, you know." With a subtle nod to Holly, she acknowledged, "Some women know to pick only the best."

"She's right," Holly whispered as his mother drifted away. She looked up at him with so much emotion filling her emerald gaze that Clay could almost convince himself it was love. "You are the best."

Guilt slammed into him, blindsiding him, just as it had when he first saw Holly floating down the staircase, looking so incredibly beautiful, and yet so vulnerable, in the glorious wedding dress.

Until that moment, he'd had himself fooled, convinced he was doing the right thing, making amends for the part he'd played in Hopewell House's closing, giving Holly the chance to foster the little boy she so obviously loved, and giving Lucas the home and family he deserved. But it was a load of bull. And he'd known it the moment his eyes met Holly's down the rose-petal-strewn runner.

He loved her.

The stunning revelation had left him dizzy, shaken and fully aware of how much he had to lose.

"Clay?" The soft touch of her hand against his arm broke into his thoughts. "Are you all right?"

"Holly, I…" Clay swallowed. He couldn't tell her, not yet, not when the truth was still so new and his emotional footing so shaky. Later, when he felt more certain of himself…and her. Later, when their relationship was strong enough to withstand the lie, then he would tell the whole truth. For now, he could only show Holly how much he loved her.

He swallowed. "What do you think about getting out of here?"

Holly smiled. "I thought you'd never ask."

The ride to the hotel passed in a blur. Holly couldn't wait to reach their destination. Anticipation thrummed in time with the limo's powerful engine. Snuggled against Clay's side, she inhaled the scent of his cologne combined with the limo's rich leather interior and the rose still tucked into his lapel.

"The ceremony was beautiful," she murmured.

So much more than what she'd expected when she and Clay had discussed getting married by a justice of the peace.

"It wasn't too overwhelming?"

Was it the presence of the minister and Clay's family that had made the wedding seem so…real? Or would she have felt the indescribable connection if the service had taken place at city hall? Most likely she would have, Holly decided.

The wedding had felt real because in her heart, it *was* real. Clay was her husband, and she loved him. But her head warned against feeling too much, caring too much…wanting too much.

When someone offered you the world, you didn't demand the sun and moon as well.

"It was perfect," she told him sincerely as she lifted her head from his shoulder to meet his eyes. "I couldn't have asked for anything more."

It must have been a trick in the passing streetlights that, for just one moment, disappointment darkened Clay's eyes. The pale glow shifted, and the more familiar spark of desire lit his blue eyes.

"Don't forget, the night is far from over. There's more to come." He brushed a kiss over her lips and sent a shiver from her head all the way down to her satin-clad toes. "Much more."

And Holly knew that, too, would be absolutely perfect.

By the time the limo reached the hotel, she longed to race through the lobby but doubted her trembling legs would support her. Instead, she walked sedately, if a little shakily, with Clay's muscular arm anchored at her waist. Paying far less attention to the opulent decor than she had the night of his party, she said, "The Lakeshore Plaza seems to be the place of firsts for us."

"Our first date," he said, hitting the button for the elevator.

"Our first night as a married couple," she added.

Our first time making love. Neither of them spoke the words, but they rang between them as loudly as the elevator's bell. The doors had barely swung shut when Clay pulled her body against his and kissed her. The taste of strawberries and champagne blended with the equally ripe and intoxicating flavor of desire, and the seductive combination went straight to her head.

Only the elevator door swishing open stopped the kiss from

going on and on. As breathless as if they'd taken the stairs, Holly and Clay stepped into the hallway.

"Here," he said, reaching into his jacket pocket and pulling out the room's key card. "Hold on to this. I'm going to need both hands free."

Holly didn't have time to ask why before he lifted her into his arms. She muffled a startled squeal against his shoulder as she threw her arms around his neck. He chuckled and strode down the hall. A little dizzy and a lot turned on, she still protested, "You don't have to carry me!"

"What kind of groom would I be if I didn't carry my bride over the threshold?" His words were teasing, but his gaze serious. Once again, Holly was struck by the notion that the wedding and the time-honored traditions meant more than either she or Clay would admit.

"This is it."

Holly nodded; he was right. This was it. Her chance for a family, for true happiness, and she wasn't going to mess it up.

"Holly?" His forehead wrinkled. "The door?"

"Oh, right." Realizing he'd stopped walking, she slid the key card into the lock, pushed the door open, and gasped. Dozens of roses filled the room, crystal vases covering every flat surface. Clay lowered her to the floor, but she stayed within his embrace. "Oh, Clay! This is wonderful."

Reaching out, he plucked a long-stemmed red rose from the nearest vase. "In my mind," he said, handing her the rose, "I always see you surrounded by flowers."

The romantic image touched her. She lifted the trembling bloom to her nose. Her free hand skimmed across his chest and stilled. "You do?"

Clay nodded, then grinned. "Of course, you're usually naked."

Holly tapped him on the shoulder with the flower, laughing, but his words sent a curl of desire threading through her. After tossing the rose onto the bed, she untied his bow tie and asked, "What else have you been imagining, Mr. Forrester?"

"Well, Mrs. Forrester," he said, reaching up and pulling the pins from her hair, "in my dreams, your hair is always down."

Feeling sexy, desirable, Holly shook out her shoulder-length curls. She slid the tuxedo jacket down his arms and tossed it in the general direction of the armchair. "What else?"

His blue eyes darkened to midnight as she worked on his shirt's onyx studs. Each loosened button exposed naked skin. His throat, then his collarbone. Dark, softly curling hair covered his chest, which narrowed as it arrowed downward. The backs of her fingers brushed his abdomen, and Clay sucked in a quick breath.

By the time he got around to answering her question, his voice came out a husky whisper. "This is good for starters."

"Starters?" Holly echoed. She tugged the tails of his shirt from his trousers and pushed the shirt from his broad shoulders. "What comes next?"

Judging by his barely suppressed smile, Clay was biting back a sexy comment. He reached behind her, trying to undo the wedding gown's buttons. He frowned and stepped around her. Running a hand down the long line of pearl-sized buttons, he said, "Tell me this thing has a zipper."

"Nope." Holly leaned her head back against his chest, letting her hair tease his skin. She'd never thought of herself as a temptress, but Clay's mounting frustration gave her an added confidence.

"Holly." He groaned her name, and the warm breath brushing her temple grew more and more ragged. As he worked on the buttons, she felt his hands shaking against her skin, and suddenly, he wasn't the only one tempted. Each tug at the bodice sent the material chafing against her breasts, and she couldn't wait to feel those hands, that breath against her.

"Hurry, Clay."

"I'm trying." The bodice loosened gradually, and she managed to take her first deep breath in hours. He stopped to knead her shoulders, his long fingers curving over her collarbones, his fingertips feathering over the upper curves of her breasts.

His touch drew out a restless yearning, and Holly tugged at the long lace sleeves. With her arms freed, the weight of the bodice drew the dress down to puddle around her feet. Dressed only in her bra, panties and stockings, she turned to Clay. The white satin and lace hid very little, and when his eyes touched on those intimate spots, a shiver raced through her. He smiled when he spotted the lace garter encircling her thigh and ran his fingers along the ruffled lace. "Wasn't I supposed to take this off with my teeth and toss it to some lucky bachelor?"

Heat rushed to her cheeks. "It was one tradition I thought we should skip. Especially since the lucky bachelor would most likely be one of your young nephews."

He shook his head. "I'm a very traditional man. You might have robbed my nephews of their first garter, but I'm not going to miss out on anything."

Holly gasped when Clay dropped to his knees. True to his word, he caught the garter between his teeth. She shivered at the soft slide of satin against her skin, accompanied by the brush of his lips against the inside of her knee, the back of her calf, even the arch of her foot as he drew off the garter. By the time he stood, she had to clutch his shoulders to keep from collapsing.

He caught her waist to steady her. "No bachelors to throw it to, but we've lived up to our part of tradition."

No bachelors, Holly realized, with a touch of amazement. Now he was Clay Forrester, her husband. And she wanted to be his wife in every way. "There's only one more tradition I'm interested in," she said. "Make love with me."

Desire darkened his eyes, and Holly expected a kiss full of hunger and passion. Instead, he kissed her with a slow, languid exploration of lips and tongue. Warmth suffused her entire body, sapping her strength, and she melted against him.

A single tug at her back, and her bra fell away. With as little effort, her panties and stockings slid down her legs. His trousers soon followed. Clay ran his fingers up and down her back, tracing restless patterns across her skin. Each teasing pass made Holly long for a more intimate touch. By the time he backed her toward the bed and lowered her to the waiting sheets, she was desperate to pull him down with her, but he resisted.

Finally, *finally,* he cupped her breast in his hand, and her back arched, lifting to the indescribable pleasure. When his head lowered and his tongue following the same path, Holly sank her hands into his hair.

The tension grew, spiraling wildly, and she gasped for breath. Clay's hand slid lower, over her flat stomach. Her hips shifted, arching into his touch. Every stroke sent desire rippling through her, slight tremors that grew and grew until a tidal wave of pleasure broke over her.

Holly cried out and slammed her eyelids closed. The protective walls that had sheltered her for so long tumbled down, leaving her exposed, vulnerable…and afraid. Afraid Clay would see the love shining in her eyes and she would never see it in his.

"Holly?"

She slowly opened her eyes and looked at him. Fierce desire etched the angles of his handsome face, but tenderness touched every feature as well. "Are you all right?"

A tenderness that had done her in. The attraction she could have ignored; the sexual desire she would have denied. But the tenderness she hadn't been able to resist.

"I'm fine," she whispered, her voice hoarse with the swallowed emotion.

"When I saw you coming down the stairs…" He paused as if arrested by the memory. Emotions flickered and flared in his eyes like reflected candlelight, each one shifting too quickly for her to read. "I don't know how I got to be so lucky."

Sliding her palms up the heated skin and tensed muscles of his chest, she turned their focus from the too heartbreakingly emotional to the breathtakingly physical. Pulling his head down to hers, she murmured, "You haven't gotten lucky…yet."

She felt Clay chuckle against her mouth. She could sense a different kind of tension radiating from his body as they backed away from the emotional precipice and he sank into her kiss, then into her body.

Holly moaned at the first seductive slide of his body within her own. Desire built again, surprising her with its intensity. When she wrapped her legs around him, Clay groaned and abandoned the slow, measured rhythm.

Clinging to his shoulders, his back, his hips, she felt every muscle flex and harden beneath her hands. The ecstasy grew, spinning nearly out of control. Holly gasped his name, and he lifted his head.

Their gazes met in a moment so intimate that at the last second, when the pleasure broke over her, she had to look away. Clay groaned her name, and she found his lips in the safety of darkness. She kissed him as he thrust a final time, shuddering above her…within her, then collapsed at her side.

She was still gasping for breath when he rolled onto his back, bringing her with him. Exhausted, she snuggled against his side. Amazed by the sheer perfection of the moment, Holly had to bite back words of love. The feeling of vulnerability returned, and she struggled to reclaim their earlier teasing mood.

"I have to say, Mr. Forrester, my first night as your wife has been quite impressive. I can't wait to see what you have planned for tomorrow."

"Tomorrow?" Clay's deep laugh vibrated straight to her heart. "Tonight is far from over."

* * *

Holly was just drifting off to sleep when the mattress shifted beneath her. She snuggled deeper into the covers, cocooned by the warmth Clay had left behind. She waited for him to come back to bed, and when he didn't, she opened her eyes in time to see him pull something from his suitcase.

"What are you doing?" she murmured.

Immediately, he hid his hands behind his back and walked toward the bed. "I've got something for you."

He was wearing only silk boxer shorts, giving Holly plenty of opportunity to admire his muscular arms and naked chest. A shiver of appreciation coursed through her. "That sounds promising," she said as she sat up and tucked the sheet beneath her arms.

Bringing his hands forward, he held out a red and green wrapped present. "Merry Christmas."

"I thought we were opening presents tomorrow morning."

"It's tradition in our family to unwrap one present on Christmas Eve," Clay told her, lying back down beside her.

Holly fingered the silk bow, biting her lower lip. "What about you? I didn't get you a gift."

A sexy smile curved his lips. Reaching out, he tugged at the sheet and reminded her, "I've already unwrapped my present."

Heat suffused her body in memory of the tender way he'd stripped away her wedding dress and made love to her. He certainly treated her like a precious gift. "You've given me so much already," Holly said, the words barely making it past the lump in her throat.

In a few days, the agency would call, and they would know if they could pick Lucas up from Hopewell House and take him home. Her dream was coming true, thanks to Clay, but self-doubt circled the edges of her subconscious.

Clay swore she was everything he wanted in a wife. What had he told her that day in the flower shop? *I'll know what I want when I see it.* Certainly the take-charge, decisive attitude was very much a part of him. But they'd known each other such a short time. Could he really be so sure that she was right for him? More importantly, could *she* trust that she was?

"Holly? Is everything okay?"

Clay smoothed a curl off her bare shoulder. The simple touch did wonders, brushing aside her worries and bringing her thoughts back to the moment. "Everything's fine."

She leaned forward and kissed him. "Thank you," she said.

"You're welcome, but you haven't opened your present yet."

Holly carefully removed the bow and slid a finger beneath the taped edges, sensing his amusement as she unwrapped the present without ruining the paper. Finally, she lifted the lid on the plain white box and sifted through the loose packing. Withdrawing the ceramic figurine, she gasped. The painted carousel pony was sculpted in mid-gallop, perfectly captured to encourage a child's imagination. "Oh, Clay, it's beautiful."

"It plays music." Taking the figurine, he wound the key, and the carousel pony turned on the wooden base in time with the tinkling music. He set it on the nightstand, and together they watched the pony spin. "The first night at Hopewell House, I asked what Christmas wish Santa didn't grant you. And you said—"

"A pony." She'd blurted out the first thing that came to mind rather than admit her desire for a family. "I can't believe you remembered."

"I figured better late than never," he said.

But he wasn't late at all. He'd come along at the perfect time. If not for Clay, she would have lost Lucas for good. Now, she had the hope that the little boy would be coming home with them.

"It's perfect." She brushed a kiss across his jaw and snuggled into his arms. "I love it."

As Holly settled against his chest and drifted off to sleep,

Clay stared at the gleaming figurine. He stroked her hair as her words echoed in his mind. *You've given me so much already.*

He inhaled a deep breath, feeling guilt press heavily against him. He hadn't *given* Holly anything as much as he'd taken advantage of the situation.

Holly never would have agreed to marry him if she'd known what he'd done. He'd told himself it didn't matter; as long as he gave her the chance to foster Lucas that would be enough. And maybe if he hadn't fallen in love, it would have been. But this wasn't about saving his conscience anymore. It was about losing his heart to a woman who deserved love and happiness…and most of all, the truth.

Chapter Eleven

"What are you doing here?" Framed by the doorway, Marie stood with hands on hips and a frown on her face.

After signing the contract in front of him, Clay looked up at his assistant. "Last time I checked, I work here. Did I miss a memo?"

"Yes, the one that read Newlyweds on Honeymoon. Do Not Disturb." Marie held out her hands as if framing a sheet of paper. Dropping her arms, she said, "You and Holly should be on a beach in the Bahamas."

"Everything happened so quickly, there wasn't time to plan anything or to clear my schedule."

Even as he spoke, Clay wondered if his words sounded as much like excuses to Marie as they did to him. Not that the reasons weren't valid, but Holly had brushed aside his offer of even a short getaway.

"We can go on a honeymoon later," he told Marie.

She looked ready to argue, but the phone on her desk rang

before she had the chance. With a final disapproving glance, she left his office. A minute later, her voice came across the intercom. "Holly's on line two."

He didn't even have the chance to say hello before Holly interrupted in a verbal burst of excitement. "I just got off the phone with Catherine." Pure joy vibrated through her voice. "We've been approved!"

Thank God. The relief that poured through Clay left him weak. He sank back into the chair, with a grateful sigh. The wait for the caseworker's call had been killing him. And not just for Lucas and Holly's sake, but also for his own. "Did Catherine say when Lucas could come live with us?"

"The day after tomorrow! I can't believe all the things I have to do first. At least now I don't have to send back the car seat, after all!"

"I told you we should have redecorated the study."

"I was just so afraid to hope."

"You don't have to be. Not anymore," he vowed. "It's going to be perfect."

"All thanks to you," Holly whispered.

His hand tightened on the receiver. Now wasn't the time for the truth. Focusing on her contagious excitement, he cleared his throat and said, "About the room—"

"I'm heading for the stores right now."

"Those must be the most frightening words known to man," he teased. "Maybe I can clear my schedule."

Even as he said the words, Clay knew it wasn't possible. He had two meetings, a conference call and a stack of résumés to sort through if he ever hoped to hire a replacement for Jensen.

"No, that's okay. You can see what I've bought when you get home."

"Sure. I can do that." Clay hung up the phone, fighting the feeling of…rejection. Shoving away from his desk, he paced his office, stopping to stare at the city skyline and the swirling snow drifting down to the busy street below. That was crazy. *He* was the one who couldn't get out of work, the one who couldn't be there.

Like he'd never been there for Victoria. But just like Victoria, Holly didn't really need him. Victoria had found another man, and Holly, well, soon she would have Lucas.

Clay wanted to be happy about that. Dammit, he *was* happy about it. But he also wanted to be part of it. And he would be, he vowed. He wasn't going to make the same mistake he'd made with his first marriage. With that thought firmly in mind, he reached for his jacket.

"Clay?" Marie's voice broke in over the intercom. "Mr. Westfell's here."

The pressure of changing his father's legacy, of changing the company's reputation, settled heavily on his shoulders. Shopping for Lucas's room was just a small step in the road toward the three of them becoming a family. He'd be there for the other more important steps. He *would* be.

"Send John in, Marie."

Clay stepped inside the penthouse that evening, greeted by the odor of paint. After the extensive remodeling at his office, he certainly recognized the smell. "Holly?"

"In here, Clay."

Her voice echoed down the hallway. He followed the sound and stopped short. His study, with its mahogany desk and matching bookcases, its leather chair and imported rug, was gone. In its place was a room perfect for a little boy.

Stunned, Clay looked at the bright blue walls, the race car border zooming across the room, the white dresser, and the matching shelves, loaded with toys and thick wooden puzzles. Parked in the center of the room was a bed in the shape of a shiny red race car.

Standing beside the bed, dressed in faded jeans and a sweatshirt, her hair caught in a ponytail, Holly met his gaze with a smile. "Surprise!"

"You did all this?"

Nodding, she wrapped her arms around her waist, happiness threatening to lift her off her toes. "I saw the bed and shelves a few days ago. The store delivered and, for an extra fee, moved the other furniture into storage."

"And the paint and the wallpaper?"

"A trip to the home-improvement store and some speed painting." Laughing, she lifted her hands to show him the hint of blue beneath her fingernails. "I couldn't wait to get everything ready! So, what do you think?"

He was amazed at the whirlwind remodel but couldn't help thinking about the rest of the apartment and how every other room, including their bedroom, remained unchanged.

Oh, sure, Holly had hung some shirts and skirts in the closet and placed some sweaters and jeans in a drawer or two. The carousel pony he'd given her decorated the top of the dresser. An extra toothbrush claimed a spot in the holder, and makeup occasionally cluttered the bathroom vanity.

But as in her old place, very little of her personality, very little of *Holly,* existed in the apartment. Knowing she didn't own the childhood mementos or family heirlooms most people possessed, he hadn't thought anything of it.

Until now. Until he saw the way she'd gone all out to put such an obviously personal stamp on Lucas's bedroom.

This is why she married you, a dark voice reminded. He was merely the means, and fostering Lucas the end. He'd known that from the start, so it couldn't possibly be disappointment leaving a bitter taste in his mouth.

"Clay?" Holly's hesitant voice broke into his thoughts. "Is everything okay?"

Forcing a smile, he said, "Fine. The room's amazing. Lucas will love it. Heck, I love it."

"Uh-oh. Are two going to fight over who gets the race-car bed?"

"I'll try to play nice. You know, seeing the great job you've done on this room, why don't you tackle the rest of the apartment, too?"

Her eyes widened. "Oh, Clay, I don't know."

"It's a bigger job, but like I said before, you can hire a decorator. Do whatever you want," he encouraged, desperate for Holly to claim some part of their home, their marriage, other than Lucas.

"But the apartment's so perfect, so *you,* just the way it is. I really can't see changing it."

Great, Clay thought. The bedroom was perfect for Lucas, the apartment perfect for him. But why wouldn't Holly claim any of it as her own?

Holly watched as Lucas wandered around the bedroom, a light blue blanket with a ragged edge trailing after him. Uncertainty tempered wide-eyed curiosity, and he hesitated, with one hand reaching for a plastic race car. He glanced over his shoulder to where she and Clay stood in the doorway.

"Go ahead, Lucas," she said. "It's all yours."

And he was all theirs. Happiness filled Holly with such iridescent warmth, she was surprised she didn't glow in the dark. Until today, the room had had a hushed, anticipatory feel, as if breathlessly waiting. The wallpaper race cars had been paused just before the finish lines; plastic dinosaurs had been crouched, frozen in mid-attack; black-and-white coloring books had waited for bright crayon scribbles. Everything had been ready and waiting.

Only with Lucas there did it seem real. All the planning, all the hoping had been realized in the blond-haired, blue-eyed boy.

"I can't believe this is happening." Turning toward Clay, Holly threw her arms around his neck and kissed him with all the joy and happiness bubbling up inside her. He'd made her dreams come true, and she loved him so much. He was like her own personal fairy godfather and Prince Charming rolled into one. Chuckling at her exuberant passion, he lifted her off her feet and spun her around in a tight circle.

"It still doesn't seem real," she murmured when he set her back on her feet.

"It's real," Clay insisted, his expression intense. "It's all real."

Holly sensed he was trying to tell her something more, but Lucas interrupted before she had the chance to dig deeper. "Look, Miss Holly!"

With his hands braced on the red car, Lucas pushed it around the hardwood floors, stopping only when the toy ran headlong into the dresser. "Car crashed!"

Tearing herself away from Clay's compelling gaze, she stepped inside the bedroom and knelt down beside Lucas. "I saw. Maybe we need your fire truck to come help."

"Okay!" Lucas thrust the car at Holly and ran over to grab the fire truck off the toy shelf.

Standing in the doorway, Clay watched Holly and Lucas play in the vivid world of make-believe. He'd never seen her so happy. She looked truly carefree for the first time, the shadows of the past swept away, memories of an unhappy childhood replaced by the desire to give Lucas the happiest childhood possible.

They were going to be a family, all three of them, Clay vowed. And when the time was right, he would tell Holly the truth—about everything.

Lucas chased Holly around the room, racing the car and the fire truck until he lost control on a tight curve, spun out of control, and crashed into Clay's foot.

"Uh-oh!" Lucas looked up, his eyes wide. A slow, mischievous smile spread, dimpling his cheeks. "Crashed some more."

Wanting to join the fun, Clay said, "Looks like you need to make a pit stop."

Confusion wrinkled the boy's forehead. "Wha's that?"

"Well—" Clay reached down and picked Lucas up "—a pit stop is when you lift the car into the air and rotate the tires." He jiggled the little boy, making him laugh. "Then you put the car back down, and the driver's rarin' to go."

"If he doesn't lose his lunch first," Holly said as he set Lucas back on his feet.

"He's fine," Clay reassured her.

Proving his words, Lucas rushed over to the shelves and held out a toy tricycle. "Here, you play with this."

"Gee, thanks, Lucas," Clay said.

Holly chuckled as Clay accepted the toy and sank down on his heels to play. "I guess you're not ready to drive yet."

Holly lifted the tiny blue sweatshirt off the pile, then bit her lip indecisively. *Maybe the red.* Kneeling in front of Lucas, she tried to smooth his tousled hair, but she'd dressed and undressed him so many times, static cling stood the blond curls on end. Judging by the pouting frown on his face, he was sick of it.

"Holly, are you almost ready? My mother will be here soon." Clay's voice drifted down the hall to Lucas's bedroom, adding to Holly's panic.

"Almost," she called back.

"Holly, did you hear—" Clay stopped short in the doorway, his gaze taking in the clothes scattered outside the closet. "What are you doing?"

"I wanted Lucas to wear the outfit your mother sent, but it's too big, and she's going to think I don't like it, even though I do. And now I can't find anything else."

Bending down, he scooped up the red sweatshirt emblazoned with a puffy airplane. "What's wrong with this?"

Holly had considered that outfit, only to reject it. Now she couldn't remember why. "It's fine, I guess."

"Do you want me to help get Lucas ready while you check on dinner?"

"No, I can do it."

She sensed more than heard his frustrated sigh. "My mother's coming for dinner. It's no big deal."

After accepting the clothes, she pulled the sweatshirt over Lucas's head…again. "Sorry, sweetheart," she said when he cried in protest. "We're almost done."

"As soon as you're dressed, we can play with your trucks," Clay promised.

The fussing stopped as quickly as it had started. With one blink, potential tears disappeared. "San'a gave me a truck."

"He did?" Clay asked, with feigned surprise. The topic set Lucas off on a running monologue about trucks: fire trucks, dump trucks, trash trucks. It was enough of a distraction for Holly to finish dressing him, but not enough to keep her own concerns at bay.

"It *is* a big deal," she said as Clay offered her his hand. Standing, she added, "This is the first chance your mother will have to spend time with Lucas."

"And she's going to love him."

Holly couldn't mimic his optimism. Jillian Forrester was still adjusting to their marriage. Now, suddenly, Clay was opening his home to a foster child. "I'm sure your mother doesn't understand."

"My mother thinks Lucas is lucky to have us, but I told her we're the lucky ones."

He flashed her a quick wink, and her heart stumbled. She loved him, so much it frightened her. If she'd thought being married, sharing his life on a daily basis, might reveal some hidden fault, some undeniable proof that he was too good to be true, she'd yet to discover he was anything less than real. He was perfect and she… She couldn't figure out why he'd married her.

"You look scared to death," Clay said.

Lucas had wandered off in search of toys. His head was buried in the toy box, and Holly half expected him to fall right in. He was so adorable, so sweet, and she couldn't stand the idea that he might ever fear he wasn't good enough. "Maybe the sailor suit would be better."

"Holly, stop!" Clay commanded. "This has nothing to do with clothes. Now, are you going to tell me what's bothering you?"

She shook her head. "You don't know what it's like, trying so hard to be smart enough, pretty enough, funny enough." *Trying so hard to make someone love you,* she thought, swallowing against the ache in her throat.

His expression softened, and he touched her cheek. "Lucas doesn't have to do anything, and my mother's going to love him. She isn't going to reject him. I promise."

She should have known he'd correctly read her worries. It was ridiculous to equate this dinner with those long-ago visits by prospective parents, but the slow roll of nerves upending her stomach felt the same.

"I know, but—" The ring of the doorbell interrupted before Holly could explain her fears. It was just as well. Verbalizing her worries would only make her nerves worse.

"Hey, Lucas, come on," Clay called to the little boy, who was still digging through the toy box. "Let's go see Grandma."

Holly blinked at the title. Elegant, refined Jillian Forrester hardly fit the image of a beaming, rotund grandma. Then again, Holly knew she wasn't Jillian's idea of a daughter-in-law.

Lucas glanced over his shoulder before he went back to excavating the toy box. "I'll get Lucas while you let your mother in," Holly said.

"Don't worry. Everything's going to be fine."

The words echoed in her mind as she helped Lucas find the truck he'd been searching for. As she picked up the rest of the toys and clothes, she heard Clay greet his mother. Lucas looked toward the doorway, his blue eyes curious. "Who that?"

Not quite ready to refer to Jillian as "Grandma," Holly said, "Let's go see."

In the foyer, Jillian was handing her coat and gloves to Clay. As always, the older woman's style and grace impressed Holly. Dressed in a pair of black silk pants and a royal blue cashmere sweater, her blond hair swept back to reveal elegant features, Jillian possessed a confidence and poise that Holly admired but could never emulate.

"Hello, Holly. It's good to see you again," Jillian said, her tone polite if distant.

"You, too," Holly said, offering a weak smile.

"And this must be Lucas." Jillian reached out to touch Lucas's blond curls, and Holly fought the urge to pull the little boy away, to shield him from the rejection she had suffered as a child.

"Lucas, can you say hi?" Clay encouraged.

Lucas hid his face against Holly's shoulder, but he opened and closed his hand in a shy wave. Jillian smiled, her expression softening. "Hello, Lucas."

Feeling the need to defend Lucas's reticence, Holly said, "Sorry. He's just a little shy around strangers."

The minute the words were out of her mouth, heat rushed to her face. "I mean—"

"I understand," Jillian broke in smoothly. "This has all happened so quickly. We haven't had the chance to get to know each other."

At the reminder of the rushed wedding, Holly thought her face might burst into flames. Clay dispelled the awkward silence with an offer to show his mother Lucas's room.

Looking around, Jillian ran a hand over the polished dresser. "How wonderful," she said, sounding genuinely impressed. "It's the perfect room for a little boy."

"Thank you," Holly responded, trying to ease the tension pulling at her shoulders.

"You did this all by yourself?" asked Jillian.

"All by herself," Clay echoed.

"That must have been a lot of work," Jillian replied.

"I enjoyed it. Really," Holly insisted, wondering if she'd imagined an unfamiliar edge in his voice.

It was with a touch of relief that she walked back to the living room, where Jillian settled onto one of the chairs. Clay and Holly sat side by side on the couch as Lucas crawled beneath the coffee table to play with his truck.

"Holly and I wanted to thank you for the outfit you sent Lucas."

"It's a little big," Holly interjected. "But he'll grow into it in no time."

"I remember when Clay was little. I had to give clothes away before he ever wore them, he grew so fast." Turning to Clay, Jillian added, "And, of course, you ate everything." Shaking her head in mock consternation, she said, "But dirt was always one of your favorites!"

"Dirt?" Holly echoed while Clay groaned.

"Oh, yes. We couldn't let him outside alone. And Anne was no help at all. Rather than stop him, she'd bring a spoon."

Holly laughed. It was so hard to picture the successful man she'd married as a troublemaking little boy.

Jillian leaned forward and confided, "Dirt was just one of Clay's phases. After that, it was bugs."

"He ate them?"

"No, I didn't eat them!" Clay burst in.

"He *collected* them," his mother said. "Every time I cleaned out his pockets, I found dozens of dead beetles and crickets."

"I don't remember any of that," Clay argued. "I think you made it up for moments like this. You really don't have to tell Holly any more."

"Oh, yes, she does!" Holly said. "It's nice to know you aren't perfect!"

His eyes caught hers. Despite the lighthearted teasing, his gaze was serious. "I never said I was perfect."

"I should hope not," Jillian said archly. "I haven't told Holly about the stunts you pulled in grade school."

Clay groaned. "Enough! Isn't dinner ready yet?" He picked up Lucas as the little boy walked by. He leaned close to whisper in his ear.

"Eat!" the boy shouted on cue.

"See, Lucas is hungry," Clay said.

"All right, dear," Jillian said. "We'll put you out of your misery. You're lucky I didn't bring pictures."

"Well, thank goodness," he said. "That would have ruined my appetite for sure."

Jillian murmured her thanks as Clay handed her a steaming cup of coffee. With Holly getting Lucas ready for bed, it was the first chance he and his mother had to talk. "Lucas seems well-adjusted to living here," she commented.

Childish laughter echoed down the hallway, and Clay said, "He's doing great, and Holly's wonderful with him." Anyone who saw Holly and Lucas together could see the love glowing in her eyes. The little boy was a dream come true. All she'd ever wanted. Clay ignored the ache at that thought and focused on the positives. "She's a great mother."

"And what about you, Clay?" Jillian asked, her knowing look confirming that she read him just as clearly now as when he'd been that bug-collecting, dirt-eating kid. "Are you a wonderful father?"

Clay longed to say yes, but the words wouldn't come. With his dimpled smile, boundless energy, and love of all things automobile, Lucas had certainly crawled into his heart, but Clay didn't feel like his father.

A barrier existed, and Holly was the one who'd thrown up the roadblocks. She was so determined to provide for Lucas's every need, to be the center of his world, the same way he was the center of hers. Clay often felt like a distant satellite, hovering at the edge of their universe.

"I want to be, but it's going to take time," he said defensively.

His mother sipped her coffee, but Clay recognized the delay tactic as she weighed her next words. "Parenting does take time and a lot of patience," she added, with a smile. "But mostly it takes love." She sighed. "Time goes by so quickly, and once in a while you might even lose patience. But I know you, Clay. You have more love to give than any man I've known."

"Clay?" Holly stepped into the study, her expression a combination of apology and bemusement. "Sorry to bother you, but I'm trying to give Lucas his bath, and well, he insists that Mr. Clay do it."

"This won't take long, Mother, if you want to wait."

Shaking her head, Jillian said, "It's time for me to go. Give that sweet boy a kiss for me, will you?"

Once his mother left, Holly turned to Clay, with confusion written in her gaze. "I tried to get him into the tub, but he wouldn't budge without you."

"It's a guy thing," Clay explained, feeling ridiculously pleased to have this one connection with the little boy. He thought it probably had to do with the night Holly asked him to watch Lucas in the tub while she took a phone call. Uncertain what to do beyond seeing to Lucas's safety, Clay had dumped half a bottle of bubble bath into the tub, creating a winter wonderland of bubbles. Ever since that night, Lucas had insisted Clay give him his nightly bath.

Lucas's eyes lit up the minute Clay walked into his bedroom. "Ready for your bath, buddy?"

"Bubbles!" the little boy shouted, scrambling to his feet and throwing his arms around Clay's legs.

"Bubbles it is," Clay agreed, swinging Lucas into his arms and flashing a wink at Holly. "One squeaky-clean kid coming up."

Half an hour later, Lucas was clean, as promised, and Clay was damp enough to have taken a bath of his own. As he carried the little boy to his bedroom, Lucas rested his baby-shampoo-scented head on Clay's shoulder. His eyes were fluttering shut by the time Clay tucked him between his race-car-printed covers.

With his mother's words ringing in his head, in his heart, Clay sank down on the bed. Running his hand over Lucas's blond curls, he whispered, "Good night, Lucas."

The boy's eyes fluttered open. "Night, Mr. Clay. Love you bunches."

It was a ritual Clay had witnessed between Holly and Lucas many nights before, but not one he'd ever participated in. Still, he knew the words, even if he did have to clear his throat to say them. "Love you more, Lucas."

He heard a soft sound from the doorway. With only a night-light illuminating the room, all he could see was Holly's silhouette and the glint of her eyes in the darkness. He stood and walked across the threshold. His words seemed to echo in a silence broken only by their breathing. She backed into the hall as he pulled the door to Lucas's room shut.

"Holly, I—"

Rising up on her toes, she kissed him, cutting off the words before he had the chance to repeat them. They caught in his throat, ache that wouldn't go away no matter how hard he swallowed.

When Holly took his hand and led him down the hall to their bedroom, he could have told her then. But the words stayed lodged in his chest. His mother might think he had a lot of love to give, but if Holly was so reluctant to accept his *help,* what hope did he have that she would accept his love?

Chapter Twelve

"Of course, I understand," Holly reassured Mary Jane's foster mother, holding the phone pressed against her shoulder while she turned the last pancake. "Lucas and Mary Jane can get together when she's feeling better."

"Is everything okay?" Clay asked once she hung up the phone. Resting one hand on her hip, he reached overhead for a coffee mug.

Holly took a moment to lean back against his chest. Mornings were one of her favorite times of the day. Clay, so gorgeous in his tailored suit, would read sections of the paper over coffee, and Lucas, sleep-tousled and adorable in fuzzy dinosaur pajamas, would sit in his high chair, eating a banana.

Evenings were better, when Clay came home to kiss a sleeping Lucas good-night before taking her hand and leading the way to their bedroom. A shiver of pleasure raced through her as she thought of nights spent in his arms. She loved falling asleep with her head resting on his chest, listening to the steady beat of his heart.

"Mary Jane has the flu. She'll be fine, but I'd planned on dropping Lucas off during my dentist appointment." Turning off the stove, she moved the skillet aside. "It's no big deal. I can reschedule."

"Why don't I watch Lucas while you're gone?" Clay asked. His tone was casual, but his gaze intent as he watched her over the rim of his coffee cup.

"You can't! I mean, the appointment's in the middle of the day."

"So I'll leave work early."

"Leave early? Clay, you haven't made it home before dark in weeks!"

The moment the words left her mouth, Holly could have gladly swallowed her tongue. She *never* mentioned how hard Clay worked. Not when she had to reheat dinners beyond good taste. Not when she had to change plans or postpone weekend outings. *Never.*

She knew how important the business was to Clay. More than that, though, she'd made the vow not to expect more than he could give.

Trying to explain, she quickly said, "You're so busy, handling all of Jensen's work as well as your own and interviewing for his replacement. And you've done so much for us already."

Clay set the coffee mug down with a loud thunk. "I've done so much already?" he echoed, anger etching unfamiliar lines in his handsome face. "Why not say what you mean, Holly? I've done *enough* already. You got what you wanted, and now you don't need me to do any more. You don't need me at all."

Holly gaped at him. Aware of Lucas seated in his high chair only a few feet away, she purposely kept her voice down. "Got what I wanted? In case you've forgotten, Lucas is precisely why *you* asked me to marry you!"

Emotions flashed across his tight features, too fast for Holly to read. "I asked you because I thought we could be a family. All three of us. Instead it's you and Lucas, and I'm in the way."

His words tugged at her conscience. Was Clay right? No, that didn't make sense. She wanted to give Lucas everything her own childhood had lacked, including a mother *and* a father. To prove it, she said, "You aren't in the way, and if you can take off early to watch Lucas, that's fine."

"I can be here. What time will you have to leave?"

"Twelve-thirty. I planned to feed Lucas lunch first."

"I'm sure I could handle feeding him, but all right."

Trying to ease the tension, Holly joked, "He's on a peanut butter sandwich kick right now. Anybody could handle it."

Her words fell flat. *Little surprise,* she thought, with a touch of shame. Clay wasn't "anybody." He was her husband, and he wanted to be a father to Lucas. "Thank you, Clay, for doing this."

"You're welcome." Some of the tension eased from his shoulders, convincing Holly she'd done the right thing. "I'll see you at twelve-thirty."

Pacing the kitchen at twelve-fifteen, Holly no longer felt so certain. She had fifteen minutes until she had to leave, but she wanted to explain a few things to Clay first. It wasn't that she didn't trust him or that he wasn't good with Lucas or any of the things he'd accused her of believing. But he'd never watched Lucas alone before.

Lucas had a favorite teddy bear he took to bed. He always wanted to read a book before he went down and liked to have music on during his nap. And he had to go to the bathroom first, even if he said he didn't need to, or he'd have an accident and wake up crying and inconsolable, remaining that way even after a change of clothes.

Grabbing the phone, she dialed Clay's number at work, but

the call went straight through to voice mail. Marie was likely at lunch, and Clay, well, he could be on his way. Or he could be in a meeting, an interview, on a conference call....

"Look, Miss Holly," Lucas announced, holding up a paper with purple and green marker scribbled in wild circles across the page. "It's for Mr. Clay to take to work."

He'll have plenty of time to look at it there, she thought, only to immediately push aside her resentment. It was her own fault. She'd expected too much. Fighting a sense of disappointment, along with an underlying feeling of justification, Holly knew she'd done the right thing in taking full responsibility for Lucas, despite Clay's protests.

"Hey, Lucas, do you want to go visit Miss Eleanor and Miss Sylvia?"

Only two children remained at Hopewell House. Soon the Hopewell sisters would be moving to Florida, and it would be good for Lucas to see them before they left.

Lucas's blue eyes lit with excitement, but then his adorable features pulled into a comical frown. "But I thought Mr. Clay was comin' home to play with me."

Great. She'd wanted to prepare the little boy so he wouldn't get upset when she left for her appointment. Instead, she'd raised his hopes and set him up for disappointment. "I know, Lucas, but I think Mr. Clay had to stay at work."

Lucas was still pouting minutes later as Holly pulled on his jacket and the mittens he hated to wear.

"You'll have fun," she promised him. "And I'll pick you up in just a little while."

After slipping into her own coat and hooking her purse over her shoulder, she took Lucas's hand in hers, opened the front door, and froze.

Clay stood on the other side of the threshold, keys in hand. His gaze cut from the purse on her shoulder to a bundled-up Lucas. "Going somewhere?"

Heat flooded her face. "I, um—"

Lucas tugged at her hand. "See, Miss Holly, I tol' you Mr. Clay was comin' home to play with me."

Holly swallowed hard. "So you did!" she replied, her tone falsely bright. "Why don't you go ahead and take your jacket off, Lucas?"

"Okay, an' I wanna show Mr. Clay my picture." He tossed aside his jacket and raced toward the kitchen.

Holly bent to retrieve the jacket, but Clay snatched it off the floor before she had the chance. Shrugging his broad shoulders, he jerked off his own jacket and hung up both garments. "If you wanted to leave earlier, you could have told me this morning."

"I—I know," she admitted. "And I tried calling, but you must have already been on your way."

"Well, I'm here now," he challenged.

"Right." Holly hesitated. She'd been ready to run out the door a few seconds ago, and now she couldn't make herself move. "I won't be gone more than two hours."

Clay simply watched, waiting.

"Lucas already had lunch. He should be ready for his nap soon. He'll want his teddy bear."

"The one the Hopewells gave him, I know," he interrupted. "He'll want to read a book first. Probably the one about the firemen. And he likes the night-light on, even though it isn't that dark." With tension drawing back his shoulders and his fists jammed in his pockets, he went on. "I'll turn the CD player on and make sure he uses the bathroom first, even though he'll say he doesn't need to. When he wakes up from his nap, he'll ask for a cookie, but he gets fruit and juice." Finally, he stopped, but he'd said more than enough.

Holly flinched at the hurt and disappointment in his expression. "Clay, I'm sorry. I didn't mean to—"

"You'd better go. You don't want to be late for your appointment."

"Forget the appointment. I can cancel."

"Right. So you can stay with Lucas."

"No!" With her explanation making matters worse, she repeated, "I'm sorry."

"So am I, Holly. So am I." Clay ran a hand over his face, seeming to wipe away the anger, leaving behind a tired resignation. "Remember the day I went to Hopewell House? You didn't want me getting too close to the kids, because you were trying to protect them. I get that. But who are you protecting now?"

Clay's question still ran through Holly's thoughts days later. She *had* kept Clay at a distance, and his accusation rang loud and clear between them. *You got what you wanted, and now you don't need me.*

"Miss Holly, I foun' my shoes!" Lucas ran into the kitchen, his blond hair flapping against his forehead and one sock slipping off his foot. He dropped the shoes to the wood floor, with a clatter.

"All right. Let's finish getting dressed."

Barely focusing on the task, Clay's words echoed in her mind, but they were no longer true. She had got what she'd *thought* she wanted—marriage to Clay and the chance to adopt Lucas. Contrary to his words, it wasn't enough, but the *more* she wanted was the one thing he'd told her he couldn't give.

His love.

She'd told herself from the start it wouldn't matter, that she could accept what he had to give and not ask for more. But every day that went by, she wanted more… She wanted everything. And she couldn't help wondering why Clay didn't. Why he was so willing to settle for less? To settle for…her.

She remembered the explanation he'd given when he

proposed—that she made him remember all the important things he'd taken for granted, that he wanted the three of them to be a family, that he wanted her in his life.

Holly wanted to believe that, but at times, dark doubts swirled like clouds preceding a storm, and she worried about some other, unrevealed, reason.

"I wanna go to the playground," Lucas told her the minute she finished tying his shoes.

"I don't know. It's pretty cold out." Holly was trying to think of a substitute activity when the doorbell rang. "I wonder who that is?"

"Let me see!" He took off for the front door, and Holly followed at a slower pace. He tugged on the doorknob, leaning back with all his weight before protesting, "It's locked."

Holly turned the lock and let him pull the door open. Her breath halted when she saw Catherine Hopkins standing in the hallway, and Holly's emotions soared. Had Lucas been cleared for adoption? Was today the day he'd officially become theirs? "Catherine, please come in. Can I take your coat?"

The caseworker shook her head. "I'm on my way into the office, so I can't stay long." She offered Lucas a small smile. "Hi, Lucas."

Holly's grip tightened on the door frame, dread slowly replacing anticipation. She'd seen that expression on the caseworker's face before. Like a slow-motion replay of a disaster, it was the same look of regret and disappointment as when the other woman had told her she hadn't been approved to foster Lucas.

"Lucas…" Holly's voice broke on his name. "Why don't you go play with your trucks for a while? I have to talk to Ms. Hopkins."

"Then can we go to the playground?"

Holly glanced down at his pleading eyes. "Sure." She cleared her throat. "Anything you want, sweetheart."

Lucas's shoes pounded the wood floors. Holly waited for the sound to stop before turning back to the caseworker. Wrapping her arms around her waist, as if she could somehow protect herself from the emotional blow, she asked, "What happened?"

Catherine shook her head. "We've located Lucas's father."

"I thought Lucas's father and his family wanted nothing to do with him." Holly didn't have to worry about keeping her voice down: she couldn't manage more than a whisper past the ache in her throat.

"That's what his mother said, but it wasn't true. Lucas's mother kept his birth a secret for the first year of his life. Once she told her ex-boyfriend about Lucas, his father and grandmother wanted visitation rights. But before they could put a case together, his mother took Lucas and left the state."

"But if she wanted Lucas, why abandon him?"

"Laura, Lucas's paternal grandmother, thinks it wasn't so much that his mother wanted him but that she didn't want Laura to have him."

The child Holly loved as if he were her own was nothing more than a pawn to his own mother.

"Laura and Lucas's father had been looking along the West Coast. Lucas's mother had lived in California all her life, so they focused the search there. Unfortunately, the only picture Laura could find was taken when Lucas was a year old."

Reaching into her purse, Catherine pulled out a piece of paper and passed it to Holly. She forced her trembling hands to unfold the poster. The photo was a snapshot of a toddler seated in a high chair. He hardly had any hair, and his face had a baby's roundness. Large letters jumped out at her. MISSING! The child's statistics were printed below the picture.

"Daniel Ryan Page," Holly read out loud.

"His mother lied about quite a few things, which is why our search for his family took so long."

Holly had prayed the search was taking so long because there was no family to find. Each day her hope had grown. She had looked forward to the day when Lucas was cleared for adoption.

The caseworker's voice came to her from far away. "Lucas came up as a possible match, and Laura came to Chicago on the chance he was her grandson."

"She's here now?" Holly asked, hollow inside.

"She's been waiting a long time to find him."

So have I! Holly raged. *He's everything I've ever wanted and never hoped to have. He's not Daniel! He's Lucas… He's my son!*

But he wasn't, and now he never would be.

"Holly, I'm so sorry."

"I have to call Clay."

The caseworker started to speak but seemed to change her mind. She took the poster and said, "I'll let you know when." She let herself out, the sentence hanging long after she'd gone. *When they'll take Lucas away…*

"No!" The word broke from Holly with a sob. She pressed her hands to her mouth, as if stopping the sound might somehow stop the pain.

"Miss Holly, can we go to the playground now?" Lucas's voice drifted down the hall.

There was no stopping the pain. It went on and on, deeper and deeper, until there was nothing else to feel. Hurt swallowed up every other emotion, a black hole sucking the life from her universe.

That darkness swarmed the edges of her vision, and Holly blinked hard to keep it at bay for now. For the time she had left with Lucas. Taking a deep breath, she wiped the tears from beneath her eyes. She waited until she walked to his room to answer. "Sure we can. We can do anything you want."

"Really?" Dimples flashed in his cheeks.

Holly reached down to touch the faint indentations—there when he smiled, gone when he didn't. "Today's a special day," she told him. "A day to remember forever."

Clay dropped an ice cube into his Scotch and water. He rarely drank, but he'd tired of pacing the living room and staring at his watch after the first hour. Another hour later, and it was all he could do not to go looking for Holly. Only he didn't know where to search. He'd already called the Hopewells and his family. No one had seen her.

Hearing the rattle of keys, Clay rushed to the front door. He yanked it open, pulling the knob from Holly's hand. "Where have you been?"

Her surprised expression turned remote, and it was Lucas who answered, his cheeks rosy from the cold. "We went to the playground an' a toy store an' McDonald's. See what Miss Holly bought me?" The little boy held up a plastic yellow airplane.

Clay managed a smile. Children were so resilient. A ride on a merry-go-round, a hamburger and plastic toy, and all was well. Silently, Holly stripped off her coat and bent down to unsnap Lucas's jacket. As she hung up their garments, Clay watched her run a hand down the blue nylon. She ducked her head, defeat weighing down her shoulders, and his fury fell away, leaving him helpless and afraid.

Lucas was rubbing an eye with his free hand and yawning, so Clay said, "With all that running around, I bet you're tired. Why don't I put you down for a nap and—"

"I'll do it!" Holly snapped, panic undercutting the defiance in her tone.

"All right," Clay said evenly. "Lucas, I'll see you when you wake up from your nap. We'll play with your airplane."

"Okay." Lucas tucked his hand in Holly's, and they disappeared down the hall.

When she didn't return within a few minutes, Clay pictured her sitting at Lucas's bedside, waiting for him to fall asleep, not wanting to waste a precious second. He returned to the den and his abandoned drink.

Holly found him there a few minutes later. "You're home early."

"I got a call from Catherine, who seemed to think I had already heard from you."

Once he'd gotten beyond his shock at the caseworker's words, Clay had tried to contain his anger. He still wasn't sure what made him angrier: that Catherine had broken the news to Holly without him there or that Holly hadn't bothered to call him at all. "You should have called me, Holly."

She stared out the window rather than face him. "There's nothing you can do."

Anger flared again, a deflection for the pain he felt. "I still deserve to know. I might not have the same claim to Lucas as you do, but it doesn't mean that I don't love him, too!" He crossed the room and caught Holly by the shoulders, forcing her to face him. His anger faded when he saw the tears in her eyes.

"I thought he was ours." Her voice broke on the words. "I thought we could keep him, but it was just a dream." She waved a hand, dismissing more than the apartment. Dismissing their entire life together. "It was all a dream."

Panic tightened his gut. "You're wrong." His fingers tightened on her upper arms, and he forced his tense muscles to relax. "These last few weeks have been real."

"Real?" She laughed, but hysteria tinged the sound. "You had the chance to play hero by marrying me, and you couldn't resist. You rode in like a white knight and saved the damsel in distress, but that's pure fantasy."

"What I feel for you is real. Our *marriage* is real!"

She shook her head, denying his words…denying his

feelings. "You married me so I could adopt Lucas. Now that we aren't adopting him—"

"Don't!" He cut her off before she could say the words. He spoke quickly, hoping logic could sway her. "You're upset, and you're hurting, but pushing me away isn't going to help."

"Nothing's going to help," she shot back.

The tears she had been fighting spilled over. Holding his breath and half-afraid she would reject him, Clay pulled her into his arms. She melted into his embrace, fisting her hands in his shirt and crying against his chest. Ragged sobs wracked her shoulders, and her hot tears seared his soul. "He was ours, Clay. He was ours!"

"I know, Holly," he said, rubbing his hand up and down her back. He helped the only way he could—holding her while she cried.

Chapter Thirteen

"Now, Lucas." Holly bent down and tugged the zipper to the boy's chin. She had to clear her throat to speak. "You be a good boy for your grandma Laura."

Confusion clouded the little boy's eyes. "Are you crying, Miss Holly?"

"I'm just a little sad," she whispered.

Lucas leaned forward and gave her a hug, patting her shoulder with a dimpled hand. "Do you wanna hold my bear?"

Wiping her eyes before she pulled away, she forced a smile and tugged on the stuffed bear's fuzzy ear. "Why don't you hang on to him? Now that you're moving, your bear is going to need you to keep him company."

The boy nodded and hugged the toy tighter. After traveling from shelter to shelter with his mother, staying at Hopewell House, then living with Holly and Clay, Lucas seemed to look at this current change as another step along the way. Holly had tried to talk about the move positively, but with Catherine standing by the door, holding Lucas's tiny suitcase, she struggled to keep smiling.

Clay lifted Lucas into the air, bringing a smile to the boy's face. "You'll have so much fun in California," he said. "It's sunny there, and it doesn't get cold, like it does here. You can play outside every day."

Lucas leaned back to look into Clay's face, as if doubting his words. "I won't hafta wear mittens?"

"Nope. No more mittens." He gave Lucas a hug, then set him back on his feet.

Catherine offered them both a sympathetic smile. "It's time to go."

As Holly straightened the knit cap hiding Lucas's blond curls, the little boy said, "Love you bunches."

"I love you more." She held him in her arms one more time, praying she could wrap a lifetime of love into a single hug.

She felt Clay's hand curve over her shoulder. The urge to throw herself into his arms nearly weakened her knees, but she pushed to her feet and pulled away from his touch.

The glimmer of hurt in his eyes pierced her heart, but the ache of losing Lucas made consolation impossible. Sometimes, when Clay didn't know she was looking, she caught a glimpse of something else in his expression, a tenderness that bordered on pain. She pretended not to notice, wishing she hadn't.

She had nothing to offer Clay. She had put her heart and soul into creating a home for Lucas. She'd hoped; she'd prayed. But in the end, she had nothing but a deserted child's room for her efforts. Though perfectly decorated, the bedroom was empty and useless without the little boy it was meant for.

She felt the same way inside. After so many years of being abandoned and rejected, she should have known better. How could she have so foolishly opened her heart? Bad enough she'd mistakenly convinced herself she could be the right mother for Lucas. She wasn't about to fail again trying to prove she could be the right wife for Clay.

Lucas looked back over his shoulder as Catherine led him out the door, waiting for Clay and Holly to come with him. They walked outside together, and Holly watched the caseworker buckle Lucas into the car seat. She wrapped her arms around her waist, huddling against the cold and heartache. Lucas's face peeked out the window. She waved and kept waving long after the car disappeared out of the neighborhood…out of her life.

Holly was going to leave him. Clay stared out his office window, watching the rush-hour traffic clog the slush-lined street, but when he closed his eyes, he saw the panic in her wide eyes. He was surprised she hadn't left already. After he emptied Lucas's room, Clay had expected her to run. She probably figured she *owed* it to him to stick around for a while.

He swore and braced both hands against the window, not bothering to turn when he heard the door open.

"Clay?" Marie spoke hesitantly. "Kevin Hendrix called. Again. He says you haven't returned his messages."

The last person he wanted to talk to was the man responsible for closing Hopewell House. Guilt pressed on his shoulders, and his arms dropped to his sides. He thought of his plan to tell Holly the truth once their relationship reached solid ground. That was impossible now. Now that Lucas was gone, the foundation was so shaky, Clay didn't know where to step. One false move and his world would crumble beneath his feet.

"I won't do business with him again."

"Well, Hendrix doesn't take no for an answer, especially when he thinks there's money to be made."

"Next time he calls, put him through," he said grimly. "I'll make it more than clear."

"Okay, but just so you know, he's threatened to come down here to talk to you face-to-face."

"Even better."

Silence filled the office, but his assistant hadn't left the room. "Do you need anything else?"

"Go ahead and leave, Marie. I'll see you tomorrow."

The door clicked shut, but Clay didn't move. He almost dreaded going home, knowing one day he was going to step into the house and Holly would be gone. She cared about him. Dammit, he knew she did! He'd counted on having the time to gain her trust and earn her love, but now that Lucas was gone, time was running out.

As he drove away from the office that evening, streetlights guided the way down busy streets. Instead of going home, he headed in the opposite direction. When he pulled up to Hopewell House, he wasn't surprised to see Holly's car. He hesitated a moment, then climbed out. Standing on the porch, his breath forming a white cloud, he stomped his feet. The door opened, and the foyer's warm glow welcomed him inside.

"Mr. Forrester!" Eleanor Hopewell's eyes widened. "This is a surprise. Holly didn't mention you'd be stopping by."

"It's sort of a surprise for her as well."

"Come in." The woman shut the door behind him and hung up his coat.

Looking around the cozy interior, Clay hated the thought of the home closing. It was a place of refuge for the foster children and for Holly. The loss was one more reason to isolate herself. "How are the placements going?" he asked quietly.

"Better than expected. A few of the short-term children have been cleared to go to relatives, and most of the others have been placed with new foster families."

"And what about you and Sylvia?"

"We'll be moving to Florida for our retirement in a few weeks. But enough of that!" Eleanor exclaimed. "Let's go see Holly, shall we?"

Despite his depressing thoughts, Clay had to smile. Eleanor Hopewell spoke to him as if addressing a child. The woman led him down the hall to the parlor where he'd entertained the children, playing Santa. Instead of the half a dozen or so children there that first night, only one child sat on the couch with Holly.

Her head was bent over a large book, and Clay saw her face in profile. Her expression was more at peace, her posture more relaxed than he'd seen since the day she spoke to Catherine. She hadn't noticed him yet, and Clay almost regretted it when Eleanor exclaimed, "We have another visitor."

Holly's head snapped up, a remote expression immediately masking her true feelings. "Clay." She handed the book to the dark-haired boy next to her and stood. "How did you know I was here?"

Her tone was perfectly even, and he wondered if he had imagined the underlying defensiveness. "I didn't, but I felt like stopping by."

"That was…nice." Her words faltered slightly.

Desperation nearly overwhelmed him, but he held back the words he wanted to say, too aware of Eleanor's presence. As if sensing his reluctance to speak in front of her, Eleanor suggested, "Milk and cookies, anyone?"

"I want some!" the boy exclaimed.

"And how about the two of you?" Eleanor asked.

Clay shook his head, and Holly mirrored his response. "No, thank you."

"I have something you'll like even better," Eleanor said, reaching into an apron pocket and handing an envelope to Holly. "The mail just arrived, with a letter from Lucas's grandmother addressed to you." She met Clay's gaze with a sad smile and led the little boy from the parlor, leaving them alone.

The envelope trembled in Holly's hand. She stared at her name written across the front, almost as if she'd forgotten that the real worth was the words inside. "I think I'll wait and read this later," she told him, stuffing the letter in her back pocket.

She stared at the fire blazing in the hearth and the toys scattered over the braided rug. Clay knew she was picturing Lucas there. Taking a chance, he murmured, "Imagine Lucas on the beach, playing with a Frisbee or trying to catch the waves." Tears flooded her eyes as he cupped her cheek. "Picture him happy, Holly, and be happy for him."

"I'm trying," she whispered.

"Let me take you home."

"What about my car?"

"We'll take yours. I'll come back and get mine in the morning." Clay almost expected Holly to refuse. She'd come to Hopewell House for a reason, to find something their house didn't have. But she gave a jerking nod.

They said a brief goodbye to Eleanor, and Clay helped Holly into her coat. They didn't speak as they climbed inside her car. He pointed the heating vents in her direction and guided the car away from Hopewell House.

Holly drew the letter from her back pocket, turned the envelope repeatedly in her hands, but made no move to open it during the silent ride. He waited until he unlocked the apartment door to ask, "Are you going to open it?" He flicked on the light and dropped the keys on the front table.

"I... Sure." Holly slipped out of her coat and hung it up. She slid a finger beneath the envelope's flap and pulled out the folded paper, with a deep breath. Taking him by surprise, she held the letter out. "Will you read it?"

Touched that she'd trusted him with this final piece of their life with Lucas, Clay prayed the little boy's grandmother had somehow found the words that he lacked. Words that would somehow help Holly heal.

He skimmed the letter before beginning to read aloud.

"Dear Holly, I hope you don't mind my familiarity, but I feel connected to you by the little boy you know as Lucas and the baby I remember as Daniel. I cannot thank you and the Hopewell sisters enough. When Daniel's mother disappeared, I prayed he was safe and well cared for. From what Catherine Hopkins told me, you and the Hopewells were the answer to my prayer. Thank you for opening your heart and your home to my grandson."

He looked up. "It's signed Laura and Daniel."

Unshed tears trembled on Holly's lower lashes; she blinked, and a single tear trembled down her cheek. Her breath caught on a shaky sigh, and she looked away from him, fighting for control, struggling to bury the pain. Her tears cut into him, leaving marks as invisible as the tracks on her cheeks, but scarring just the same. And as much as he wanted to ease Holly's pain, the only thing that would help now would be to let it all out.

Clay set the letter aside and wrapped his arms around her. She went willingly, resting her head against his chest. "As much as it hurts, I'd do it all again."

The words were the most encouraging he'd heard since the caseworker took Lucas away. If Holly could get past the hurt and regret, maybe they would have a chance. "Try to remember the good times."

Sheltered in his arms, Holly didn't want to remember. She didn't want to think at all. All she wanted was the sweet oblivion of Clay's touch. She was being unfair, holding him at arm's length emotionally yet still expecting physical intimacy. But she felt so hollow and lost, and he could make that all go away, even if it was only for a short time.

"Clay, make love to me."

His shirt muffled her words, but he still heard. His body tensed as he drew back to meet her gaze. "Holly, wait—"

She didn't give him time to say more. Stretching on tiptoe, she cupped the back of his neck and kissed him. Clay froze, resisting her advances, but Holly didn't withdraw. Her parted lips caressed his as her tongue touched, tempted and teased until he gave in with a groan of surrender. Grasping her hips, he lifted her against him. His tongue plunged into her mouth, and tendrils of heat spiraled through her.

Holly waited for sensation to take over, for her mind to go blank, but it didn't happen. Thoughts of Clay filled her head. From the first moment he'd stepped into Hopewell House, dressed as Santa, he'd been so caring…so generous…even though she'd offered so little in return.

But this, this chemistry, was a gift they gave each other. They'd made love numerous times since their wedding, but this time would be different. She could taste it in the hunger of his kiss, hear it in his rough whisper of her name, feel it in the desperation of his touch.

He slid his hands beneath the hem of her sweater, his fingertips teasing the fluttering muscles of her stomach as he pulled the sweater off and tossed it aside. His gaze caressed her, and the fluttering rose until her breasts tightened and swelled within her bra.

"My turn," she whispered huskily as she tugged on his tie, loosening the knot and mimicking his actions as she drew the tie over his head.

Together, they weaved and stumbled down the hall, attention far more focused on the movement of their hands than their feet. They managed the few steps toward the bedroom before her bra dropped to the polished floor. Clay's shirt followed, and by the time they reached the bed, the rest of their clothing had fallen away.

Holly slid onto the bed and waited for Clay to join her, but instead, he stood still and stared at her. "What's wrong?" A tremor shook her words despite her best attempts to keep her voice steady.

"I was just thinking how beautiful you are."

Holly heard the wistfulness in his voice, as if he feared she might disappear. And maybe he did. After all, she hadn't made any promises, and the one time he'd tried to talk to her about staying, she'd shut him out. "Clay."

His name broke from her lips in a whispered plea, but she wasn't sure what she'd asked for. Time? Understanding? Whatever she needed, he answered the more pressing desire. The bed dipped, and he leaned over her, with both hands braced on either side of her, as he lowered his head.

Clinging to his muscular arms, Holly drank in his taste, moaning softly when he broke off the kiss to move down her body. Each caress washed away a little of the heartache, and when he pressed his lips against her heart—a kiss to make it all better— a single tear trickled from her eye and carried away her sorrow.

"Love me, Clay," she pleaded.

"I do, Holly." He lifted his head, his expression both fierce and tender. "I do."

He brushed the tear away with his thumb and carried it to his mouth, sharing in her pain. He kissed her again, the salt of her tears sharp on his tongue. When he would have caressed her to the edge of ecstasy, seducing her with hot, arousing words whispered against her skin, Holly restrained him.

With her hand on his muscled chest, she rolled him onto his back. Her lips and hands charted the same sensual course on his body that Clay had frequently discovered on hers. She felt him swallow when her tongue traced the column of his throat. Her mouth drifted lower, over his collarbones, to the center of his chest. His heart pounded wildly, matching the desire thrumming through her own veins.

He murmured her name and tunneled his fingers into her hair. His grip tightened almost imperceptibly as her open-mouthed kisses drifted lower. Finally, he lifted her to straddle his body, hard and ready for hers.

His hands guided her hips, and the loneliness faded, not in selfish sexual oblivion, but in the wonderful shared joining. Each stroke brought them close…closer…until they were one in body and in soul. The empty, hollow feeling disappeared, replaced by a sense of completion and the knowledge that finally, after all her searching, she had found where she belonged.

Clay's body strained beneath hers, reaching for pleasure just beyond grasp, and Holly clutched his shoulders. Her hands kneaded his muscles in time with the rocking rhythm of their bodies. And just as the promised pleasure broke, just as her eyes automatically drifted closed, he whispered, "Holly, look at me."

The husky plea called to her, leading her from the darkness into a light so bright that one look at the love shining from his eyes fractured her universe into a prism of color.

Her body tensed—for a moment, for an eternity—until she collapsed onto Clay's chest as he thrust and shuddered a final time. Ragged breathing combined in the silent room as Holly peppered his damp skin with kisses. His heart thundered against her lips, and she laid her head down, listening to the beat gradually slow to an even, steady rhythm.

Eventually, the hand Clay ran up and down her spine stilled, and his breathing deepened. Raising her head, Holly studied his handsome features. The dark lock of hair falling across his forehead, his straight eyebrows, the crescent-shaped shadow his eyelashes cast against his cheekbones. She traced a fingertip down his nose and stopped at his lips. Even in his sleep, he smiled.

Fragile wings of hope stirred inside her, like a butterfly trapped behind glass, longing to take flight. Holly fought the panicked urge to tamp down the tender emotion. Past experience had taught her how painful hope could be, and she had tried to take shelter from hurt by secluding herself in a place that allowed no room for hopes and dreams. But then Clay had come along to set her free. She couldn't go back to the life she'd had before. Not after Clay had taught her that living without hope wasn't living at all.

Holly woke late the next morning. She felt a twinge of disappointment as she ran her hand over the empty pillow beside her. Clay must have left for work hours ago, but he'd let her sleep rather than wake her to say goodbye.

For the first time since Lucas had left, the crushing weight in her chest eased. At some point during the night, long after Clay had pulled her into his arms and drifted off to sleep, Holly remembered the words he'd read from the letter Lucas's grandmother wrote.

You...were the answer to my prayer.

In an odd way, Laura Page had also answered Holly's prayer. As a child, she'd longed for some unknown grandmother or distant relative to rescue her from foster care. She'd imagined the tearful reunion, the words of love, the vow that they'd never stopped looking for her. And now, that childhood dream had finally come true.

Not for Holly, but for Lucas.

It would be so selfish for her to begrudge Lucas and his grandmother what she herself had wanted for so long—a family of her own. She'd had that for a little while, she and Lucas...and Clay.

What I feel for you is real. Our marriage *is real!*

She could still have that family with Clay if she didn't let her fears override the love she felt. She loved him, and it was time to tell the truth. Time, too, to find out exactly why he'd married her.

The nerves fluttering in her stomach as she stepped into the lobby of Clay's building belonged more to first date jitters than a surprise lunch with her husband, but Holly couldn't help it. She smoothed her palms over her black skirt, a reminder of how she'd taken extra time with her appearance. She'd topped the calf-length skirt with an emerald sweater, and she wore her hair loose around her shoulders the way Clay liked it.

The flower shop caught her eye, and she stepped inside, inhaling the familiar earthy, floral scent.

"Holly, how are you?" Marilyn smiled from behind the counter and set aside the long-stemmed rose she'd been trimming.

"Good. I stopped by to take Clay to lunch and had to come say hi."

"I'm glad you did. We've missed you."

"Me, too." While Lucas had lived with them, Holly hadn't had the time to think about work. But now that her days were no longer filled with crayons, games and cartoons, she missed her old job.

"Did you want to pick up any flowers while you're here?" Marilyn asked.

"Actually, I'd like a bouquet delivered tomorrow."

She selected an arrangement and picked out a tiny card. Twirling the pen, she tried to think of what to write. The match-book-sized card couldn't possibly hold everything she wanted to say. Finally, she wrote a short message. She let out the breath she hadn't realize she'd been holding and signed the card. As if the words were magic, Holly felt the doors burst open, and she was finally free to fly.

"Thanks, Marilyn."

The tinkling bell above the shop's door chimed as she left. Holly walked to the elevators and smiled politely at the well-dressed blond man who held the doors open. When she hit the button for Clay's floor, he asked, "Do you have a meeting with Clay Forrester?"

Disappointed, Holly shook her head. She'd called Marie earlier to ask if Clay was available, but something must have come up. "No, Clay's my husband. I was stopping by to say hello."

The man's sandy brows rose, and Holly sensed, with a touch of discomfort, that he was measuring her up. "That's right. I heard Clay got married over the holidays. Congratulations."

"Thank you, Mr.—"

The man shook his head at the formality. "Clay and I are old friends. Call me Kevin." He smiled. "Kevin Hendrix."

A cold fist closed around Holly's heart, and she shivered. "Hendrix?" she echoed, forcing the words past the ache in her throat. No. It couldn't be. It wasn't possible.... "As in Hendrix Properties?"

His smile flashed capped white teeth. "You've heard of my company?" He chuckled. "Nice to know advertising pays off."

Anger threatened to choke her, and she couldn't wait to get away from the man. She squeezed through the elevator doors the second they opened. Desperate to talk to Clay and hear from him that the incriminations swirling through her mind weren't true, Holly hurried past Marie's desk without responding to the woman's cheery greeting and threw the door to her husband's office open.

Clay looked up and smiled until he took his first good look at Holly. Her emerald eyes blazed, and her face was pale except for the two bright spots of anger staining her cheeks. "What's wrong?" he demanded, circling his desk and reaching out for her.

She threw up her hands as if warding off a lethal blow. "Don't touch me!"

Fear pounded in his chest, and Clay tried to keep his voice steady and soothing. "Holly, tell me what's wrong."

"Why is he here, Clay? Why is that man here to see you?"

"Who?"

Striding over to his desk, she slapped her hand down on the intercom. "Marie, tell Clay who's here to see him." Her gaze refused to relinquish his, the blame in her eyes striking with deadly accuracy.

"Um, sure." Marie's surprise was evident even across the speakerphone. "Kevin Hendrix is here."

Clay took a deep breath. "You know how I've been investing money in troubled companies to keep them from going under. Hendrix Properties was one of the companies I helped in the past."

"In the past?" Holly asked. "Like, say, a few months ago, when Hendrix decided to sell Hopewell House right out from underneath a half a dozen foster children." Her challenging expression defied him to plead his ignorance or his innocence. The anger radiating from her told Clay that neither protest would do any good, but he had to try.

"Holly, I didn't know."

"And if you had known, that would have changed everything, wouldn't it? *Everything,*" she insisted.

"Holly, listen to me," he said, fear hollowing out his gut. "I invested in Kevin Hendrix's company, and I gave him advice to turn larger homes into rental apartments. If I had known—"

"You did know," she accused. "You did! That's why you tried to find a house to replace Hopewell House. That's why you…" Her voice cracked, but she pushed on. "Why you anonymously donated money for all the children. Do you think I'm stupid, Clay? I knew it was you. I just didn't know why. I thought you sympathized with the kids' problems, but you were the cause!"

"I didn't know! And when I found out about Hopewell House, it was too late."

Holly went on as if she'd never heard him. "All the things you did, for me, for Lucas. I actually believed it was because you cared." She gave a mocking laugh. "You had me fooled. I thought everything you did was out of compassion, but it wasn't. It was to appease your guilt."

She was right, Clay admitted. Guilt had motivated his actions. At least at first. The money he'd donated had certainly been an attempt to buy off his own conscience. But making himself feel better had stopped being important. Only Holly's happiness mattered. "You're wrong, Holly. It doesn't have anything to do with me. Everything I did was for you."

"I don't believe you. You've lied to me from the start."

"I made a mistake." Clay couldn't deny that, but certainly he and Holly could get past it. They had to. "I admit I'm not the hero you thought I was. I'm a man who screwed up and did his best to make up for it."

Holly shook her head. She didn't want to hear what Clay had done to make amends. She *had* foolishly seen him as her hero. The truth cast a cynical light over his actions; he wasn't heroic, he was opportunistic, and she'd been a fool for falling for the ploy so easily. Her budding trust shriveled and died.

She'd come to the office to find out why Clay had married her; now she knew.

"Holly." He reached out and grabbed her shoulders before she had the chance to back away. "I'm sorry. I never intended to hurt you."

"You never intended for me to find out," she retorted, holding herself rigid within his grasp.

Clay tightened his grip at her unrelenting stance. Holly saw the anguish in his expression, but anger blinded her to anything beyond her own pain. "You have to believe me. You have to *forgive* me."

"This isn't about forgiveness, Clay. It's about appeasing your guilt. Go throw some money at the problem. You'll feel better."

"Don't do this, Holly," he demanded. "I did *not* marry you out of guilt. Don't let anger destroy us just because you're too frightened to trust what we have."

"Trust?" She laughed bitterly. "How can you possibly expect me to trust you?"

"Because I love you!" Clay shouted.

"Don't!" Holly jerked out of his arms. "I'm not listening to any more of your lies!" She grabbed the door handle, desperate to get out of his office...out of his life.

"Holly..."

She made the mistake of looking back.

"I love you." He repeated the words, the effect of hearing them no less devastating the second time.

She'd waited her whole life for the simple statement, but she no longer trusted Clay enough to believe him. She turned the handle and walked away, leaving her hopes and dreams behind.

Chapter Fourteen

Clay took one step into the house and knew instantly that Holly was gone. He felt her absence as strongly as the loss of oxygen. He couldn't see anything missing, but she was gone just the same. He couldn't breathe without her.

He reluctantly wandered into the bedroom. Other than an empty drawer or two and the exposed hangers in the closet, he had little proof that she'd lived there, little proof that she'd gone.

Clay dropped onto the bed and ran his hands through his hair. He'd made a mistake, thinking he should give Holly time to calm down. Instead, she'd used the time to leave. It was one screwup in a long list of screwups. The first had been hiding the truth from Holly.

He didn't even know where she was! She'd given up both her job and her old apartment once they'd married. The only friends of hers that Clay had ever met were the Hopewell sisters.

Of course. Where else would Holly go? She was furious

with him; staying at Hopewell House in the final weeks before the house was scheduled to close would be the perfect way to keep her anger alive.

A knock on the door stopped Clay's heart. Had Holly changed her mind? Would she at least give him the chance to explain? Long strides carried him down the hall, and he yanked the door open.

His mother blinked in surprise. Clay tried to hide his disappointment. "Mother, hello."

Jillian frowned. "Is everything all right, Clay?"

"Sure. Fine." The words rang hollow and unconvincing.

His mother stared at him. "Aren't you going to invite me in?"

Company was the last thing Clay wanted, but he opened the door and led the way down the hall to the living room. "Would you like something to drink?"

"No, thank you."

Clay didn't let his mother's refusal stop him from fixing a Scotch.

Jillian set her purse on the coffee table and settled into an armchair. "Where's Holly?"

"She's at Hopewell House."

A short silence filled the room. "I'm sorry things didn't work out with Lucas," she said softly, "but he'll be with his father and grandmother now. I can't imagine how that must have felt, not knowing where he was. There's nothing like loving a child." Jillian paused briefly. "Have you and Holly talked about having children?"

Clay unwittingly slammed his drink down on the end table. "Mother—"

She cut off his protest with a defensive frown. "Now, Clay, I'm your mother. I'm allowed to ask that question, and I've waited thirty years to do so."

He started to respond, only to hold his tongue. He swirled

the ice cubes in his glass. Something in his mother's words struck him, and he looked up. "When I was married to Victoria, you never asked me about kids."

His mother looked at him askance, her gaze shrewd. "You and Victoria were too young. A child was the last complication either of you needed."

"But you think Holly and I…"

Clay let the words trail off. Images of Holly cradling a baby, *his* baby, filled his thoughts. His gut clenched, and the quick swallow of Scotch he took did little to settle his stomach. He'd wanted that image to be part of his future more than anything.

"Holly wants a family as much as any woman I've met," his mother insisted.

He shook his head. "Sorry, Mother, but you're wrong. Holly didn't want a family. She only wanted Lucas."

Jillian stood and twisted her rings. "That makes no sense." She pinned him with a sharp look. "Holly is in love with you."

As much as he wanted to believe it, Clay shook his head. He'd shouted his feelings to Holly that afternoon. But if she'd returned the emotion, she wouldn't have left. "You don't understand," he told his mother. "The reason you never had the chance to get to know Holly before the wedding was because I hardly knew her. We got married so she could adopt Lucas. Now that Lucas is gone, so is Holly." There. The truth was out, the words sounding the end of their relationship.

"Are you saying *you* married Holly just so she could adopt Lucas?" his mother demanded.

"No!" Clay picked up his glass again, only to discover it was empty. He stood, but Jillian stopped him before he made it to the liquor cabinet.

"Then why, Clay?"

"Because I love her." This time he whispered the words.

Even so, his mother heard him and frowned. "And you still let her leave?"

"It's not that simple!" Clay took a deep breath and explained about Hendrix Properties, Hopewell House, and his part in its closing.

"But you didn't know," Jillian protested.

"That it was a foster home? No, I didn't," he said, but guilt tinged his words all the same. "But it was business...."

Jillian tilted her head to one side, silently studying him. Finally, she said, "You're afraid your advice would have been the same even if you had known about Hopewell House."

"I don't know," Clay said, dropping his head in anguish.

"Well, I do." Jillian took the glass from his lax hand and set it aside. "You aren't your father, Clay. You would have done what you thought was right."

You aren't your father. His head snapped up. "You knew? About Dad and the way he did business?"

His mother gave him a chiding look. "I was married to the man for thirty-five years. Of course I knew. Which isn't to say I approved." She sighed. "When your father first took over for his father, the business wasn't nearly as sound. In the first few years, he had to fight off several hostile takeovers. Despite whatever he told you about business being business, your father took that very personally. He believed his ruthless business tactics were necessary, but he tried to keep that part of his life away from you and Anne."

Except his business had played such a big part in Michael Forrester's life that he'd become little more than a stranger to his own children.

I'm just a girl... Book smart doesn't equal business smart, or so Dad always said.

Clay recalled his sister's words and her atypical uncertainty. Michael Forrester might have thought he was protecting Anne by discouraging her interest in the cutthroat business world, but he'd really been protecting himself and hurting his daughter in the process.

The same way he had lied to protect himself and hurt Holly, Clay realized, with sudden clarity.

He winced. "I've tried so hard not to be like Dad, but I've made so many of the same mistakes, not to mention repeating my own."

He'd fallen back into the habit of using business as an excuse to avoid problems in his marriage. And that was exactly what it was, what it had always been—an excuse. His first marriage hadn't failed because of the way he'd thrown himself into business. He'd thrown himself into work to avoid his failing marriage.

He needed to hire a replacement for Jensen immediately and… Clay stopped short. Damn, if the obvious answer to that problem hadn't been staring him in the face the whole time!

After running the idea past his mother, he waited for her response. Jillian smiled. "It's a wonderful idea! One that, unfortunately, your father would never have considered."

"Yeah, well…"

"Clay, do you really think you would ever put business in front of the welfare of children?"

The answer came to him from deep within his soul. Without the burden of guilt or the weight of responsibility. "No, I wouldn't."

"Well, then, you have your answer."

"Except it doesn't matter, at least not to Holly."

"Then maybe that's not the real reason why she left," Jillian mused.

"That's the reason," he stated flatly. "Thanks to my business with Hendrix, Holly hates me."

"She's scared, Clay. As you said, the two of you didn't know each other very well. Holly wanted to adopt Lucas, and you must have seemed like the answer to a prayer." His mother touched his chin. "But then she found out you were only a man. A wonderful man."

He gave a short laugh. "Believe me, that's the last thing Holly's thinking."

"Not when she found out about Hendrix, but until then, you'd swept her off her feet. She learned reality was even better than the dream, and it frightened her."

Even before Holly had learned about Hendrix, Clay had sensed she planned to leave. Maybe she had been so afraid their relationship wouldn't work out, she'd grasped the first excuse to leave. Not that Holly was the only one at fault. He'd certainly given her one hell of a reason to go.

"Talk to her," Jillian urged.

Clay eyed his mother curiously. "I didn't think you approved."

"I admit, I had my doubts," she said, "but now that you've told me everything, I believe I understand." With a chiding look, she told him, "You can't put conditions on marriage and expect a woman to love you unconditionally."

Holly stared out the window. The overcast skies, bare trees, and gray, slush-lined gutters mirrored her depressed mood. By contrast, the Hopewell House parlor, with its cheery fire blazing in the fireplace and the scent of cinnamon drifting from the tea tray, should have felt warm and homey. Somehow, though, the peace and contentment were missing.

"How long do you think you can stay here?"

Holly turned away from the parlor window to face the Hopewell sisters. Responding to Sylvia's question, she said, "I'm planning to chain myself to the front doors. Do you think that would keep Kevin Hendrix's construction crews away?"

"I think what Sylvia really wants to know is, when are you going home?" Eleanor pressed.

"I don't have a home," replied Holly.

"You have a home *and* a husband," Eleanor stressed.

Staring at the two women, who had always stood by her,

Holly crossed her arms defensively. "How can you expect me to go back there? I told you what Clay did!"

"You also told us he didn't know about Hendrix's plans until it was too late," Sylvia pointed out as she fixed a cup of tea.

"How am I supposed to believe that? How am I supposed to believe *anything* he said?"

Eleanor wrapped an arm around Holly's shoulders and led her to the couch. "What else did he say?"

Holly sank into the cushions and accepted the tea Sylvia offered. She wrapped her hands around the cup, trying to absorb the warmth. "He said he loved me," she whispered, "but he's been lying to me from the start." Painful embarrassment heated her cheeks when she remembered Clay's proposal and how her heart had leapt at the chance to say yes. She should have known he was too good to be true. How could she have foolishly believed that a man like Clay Forrester wanted to marry a nobody like her?

Sitting beside Holly on the couch, Eleanor asked, "How do you know that was a lie? Maybe Clay was telling the truth."

"No!" The cup and saucer clattered at the violent denial, and Sylvia took them from Holly's trembling hands. Huddling deeper into the cushions, she insisted, "He was lying! He doesn't love me. No one—"

"No one's ever loved you," Eleanor finished softly.

Hearing the words spoken aloud, having her darkest fear unleashed inside the cheerful parlor, Holly felt the pain build until it escaped in a gut-wrenching sob. She pressed a hand against her mouth but couldn't stop the sound. Eleanor wrapped an arm around her shaking shoulders, and Sylvia knelt beside her, with a box of tissue.

"I l-love him so much," Holly whispered, "but he doesn't... He can't."

"I would think after all the time you've spent here, you'd know better than that," Eleanor said.

After wiping her eyes, Holly balled up the damp tissue in one fist. Sniffing back tears, she said, "I know the two of you care about me."

"Of course we do," Sylvia said as she set the tissue box on the coffee table, "but I don't think that's what Eleanor meant."

Her sister sighed and shifted on the cushions to face Holly. "Clearly, Kevin Hendrix didn't respect the work we've done here, but I never thought you would devalue what we've accomplished."

"Devalue?" Holly gaped at the unexpected attack. "How could you possibly think I would do that?"

Eleanor shrugged a bit too casually. "Well, we tried to show every child who came through our doors they deserved love. No matter if they were abandoned, abused or neglected, we told them they were special. But you don't believe that."

"Of course I do!"

The words were barely out of Holly's mouth when Eleanor challenged, "And you are just as special as every child we've cared for. So why is it so hard to believe Clay loves you?"

She should have seen it coming, but the trap slammed shut, locking Holly inside, with no place to hide from her own fears. Was it possible that Clay loved her? And if he did…

If he did, she would have to trust him with her whole heart. She'd have to forget every hard-earned lesson she'd learned and believe for the first time in her life, that she was good enough, smart enough, pretty enough for someone to love.

And not just *any* someone. Clay—the man she loved, the man whose lies had already shaken the foundation of her trust.

"I can't believe you want me to come work with you!"

Clay smiled wryly at his sister's excitement as Anne claimed his chair and sat with her feet propped on his desk. "Something tells me you'll get used to the idea."

The answer to his professional problems had clicked into

place while he was talking to his mother. Anne was the perfect replacement for Albert Jensen. She might not have business experience, but she had her degree and, more importantly, the drive to prove herself.

Michael Forrester had never given her the chance, but Clay wasn't going to protect their father anymore, at least not at his sister's expense. There would be time to explain his plans later. For now, Clay wanted Anne to enjoy her newfound place in the family business.

"I should warn you," Anne said, with a sparkle in her eyes, "I'm going to do my best to steal Marie from you. Everyone knows she's the real genius."

"Steal her? Are you kidding?" Clay sat on the edge of the desk. "She'll jump at the chance to leave me." He had kept the words teasing and light, but the simple, unintentional phrase pierced his heart.

Anne swung her feet off the desk and stood. "Clay, I am so sorry. The job offer took me by surprise, but I shouldn't have—"

"It's okay." Solving his business problems was so much easier than facing the disaster of his love life. "I'd hoped you would be excited about it."

"But you shouldn't even be here. You need to go after Holly." Anne pointed at him. "She loves you, you know."

"So everyone keeps telling me." His mouth pulled into a grimace. "Everyone except Holly."

A quick knock interrupted them, and Clay glanced over his shoulder. Marie walked in, with a hopeful smile on her face and a basket of flowers in her hands. "Sorry to interrupt."

"No, please, come in!" Anne insisted.

Clay gave a short laugh as he stood but couldn't look away from the bouquet Marie set on the desk. The red carnations, the black-eyed Susans, and the few sunflowers looked like Holly.

"Well," Anne prompted, "are you going to open the card?"

"Geez," he muttered, "give a woman a job and suddenly she gets all bossy."

"Clay!" Female voices combined in an impatient demand. He could sense Anne and Marie holding their breath as he pulled out the card nestled amid the fragrant flowers.

Anticipation thrummed through his veins as he slid the card from the envelope. He stared at the handwritten words, his heart pounding. She must have ordered the flowers before she talked with Kevin Hendrix, but that didn't keep his emotions in check.

Thank you for giving me the courage to dream. Love, Holly.

"I have to go talk to her." With more hope than he'd had in days, he grabbed his jacket and pulled it on. He stopped at the threshold and glanced back over his shoulder. "Oh, and, Anne, you're in charge while I'm gone."

"Wait! I'm what?"

Clay was still chuckling at his sister's panic when he hit the button for the elevator, but he wasn't worried. He'd made the right decision with Anne. Now, he could only hope to make the right decision with Holly.

If she loved him, they could work this out. If she loved him, anything was possible.

Not sure what kind of greeting to expect, Clay took a deep breath before knocking on the front door of Hopewell House. Eleanor opened it a moment later and waved him inside. "Mr. Forrester, we've been expecting you."

Surprised by the warm welcome, he asked, "You have?"

"Ever since Holly arrived." She took his jacket and hung it up for him. "She's completely miserable," the older woman confided in a whisper.

Clay felt a touch of guilt combined with perverse satisfaction. He wanted Holly to be happy, but not happy *without* him. "Did she tell you about my association with Hendrix?"

Eleanor sighed. "She did. And I don't blame her for being upset."

"I'm so sorry I had anything to do with the house closing."

"If you want to make it up to me, make it up to her."

Clay followed Eleanor's directions and went down the hall to the last door on the left. Lifting a hand, he touched the carnation in his lapel for luck, then knocked on the door.

"Come in." Knowing Holly would have given a different answer had she bothered to ask who it was, Clay took advantage and opened the door.

Her eyes widened and locked on his. She set the book she'd been reading aside and pushed out of the rocking chair. "What are you doing here, Clay?"

Obviously, she'd expected him to let her go. And he might have if he hadn't talked to his mother, if Holly had canceled the flowers…if he thought for one minute he could live without her.

I've come to take you home. He managed to stop himself from speaking the words. "I wanted to thank you for the bouquet."

Holly flinched. "I forgot…"

"I figured as much, but it's too late now," he said. Holly had given him her love, and he wouldn't let her take it back.

"Clay, this isn't going to work," she said and sighed.

"Look, I know you're scared."

"Scared!" Bright color flooded her cheeks.

"Yes, scared. You want to stay married to me, and it frightens you."

She shook her head. "You're wrong. We got married for the wrong reasons. Staying married won't make it right."

"Holly," Clay began, but he didn't know what else to say to convince her. As he ran a hand through his hair, his frustrated gaze swept the room until a familiar object on the windowsill caught his attention. "You didn't take much with you when you left."

"None of it was mine to take."

"You didn't make it yours. That made it so much easier for you to leave." Clay crossed the room to stare out the window. His back was rigid, the straight lines of his suit in keeping with the untouchable image. Holly longed to reach out and stroke his broad shoulders one final time. Instead, she tightened her hands into fists.

"I don't want anything from the penthouse." She couldn't bear any reminders of the time they'd spent together.

"That's what I figured," he said, turning to face her. "Which is why I'm surprised you brought this with you."

Holly stared at the carousel pony he held. After packing the few belongings she'd brought to Clay's, she'd closed the dresser drawer a final time. The slight shaking of the dresser had rocked the pony enough to start the music. Listening to the melodious tune, she hadn't been able to leave the pony behind.

Clay tossed the fragile ceramic figurine from hand to hand, and Holly fought the urge to snatch it away from him. "I just… I wanted—"

"Wanted what? Not me, that's for sure." Bitterness tinged his words. "So why bother to keep this?"

Holly stared at the carousel pony, which Clay held so casually, so carelessly. "Because!" She couldn't stop the words or the tears from pouring out. "I wanted to hold on to something! I lost so much, and I needed to keep *one* thing for myself."

Clay set the carousel pony aside and pulled Holly into his arms. "I'm sorry about Lucas, and I'm sorry I ever did business with Kevin Hendrix," he whispered fervently, his lips brushing her temple. "Holly, you never lost me. You *left* me. But I love you too much to let you go, and I know you love me. If you can forgive me, I'll spend the rest of my life making this up to you. I swear, I never knew about Hopewell House."

He caught her by the shoulders, his fingers pressing into flesh, as if he could force his words to sink in through the heated contact. Weakness sapped her strength, and she melted into his embrace.

"I know you didn't." Holly pulled back far enough to wipe a knuckle beneath each eye. "But you should have *told* me." She gave a self-deprecating laugh. "Okay, so I should have known you had another reason for marrying me, but I believed you. I thought you wanted me. Instead, you were just trying to bury your guilt."

"That's not true." Clay cupped her face, his thumbs feathering across her damp cheeks. "You know me better than that. I use my money to salvage my conscience. I married you because I had already fallen in love."

"You never said that," she murmured.

"You weren't the only one who was afraid. I've never felt this way before. I was afraid to love you, afraid of what would happen when you learned the truth. I wasn't sure you'd believe that I've completely fallen for you." He tilted his head, trying to make contact with her downcast eyes. "I'm still not sure you believe me."

Holly had thought leaving Clay was the hardest thing she'd ever done, but meeting the honesty in his gaze, she knew one thing would be more difficult—staying with him. To stay would be the biggest risk she'd ever taken, but how could she not take that chance when his love was the reward?

"I do believe you." She took a deep breath and added, "And I do love you."

She let out a laugh when Clay wrapped his arms around her and spun her in a circle. He kissed her, and Holly responded with the love she'd been saving her entire life. She felt desperate for his taste and touch, as if it had been years since they last kissed. When he eventually tried to pull back, she rose on tiptoe and followed him. She molded her body to his, deepening the kiss once more. By the time they broke the kiss, she was breathless, and a sensual light gleamed in Clay's eyes.

"Holly." His voice came out hoarse, and he had to clear his throat to start over. "We've rushed through every step in our relationship. I want you to be sure this is what you want. If you need more time, I'll wait." His promised patience warred with his hungry gaze.

"Take me home, Clay," she said.

A slow smile brightened his features, but he asked, "Are you sure? You're not afraid anymore?"

"Terrified," she said and laughed shakily. "But the only thing that scares me more is the thought of living without you."

Clay touched his forehead to hers. "That's one thing you don't need to worry about. Give me the next forty or fifty years, and I'll prove it to you."

Epilogue

Holly stood on the stepladder and topped the tree with a sparkling star. "How does it look?"

Clay followed the graceful outline of Holly's body. In a room filled with colorful decorations, bright lights and golden cherubs, Holly was the most beautiful angel by far.

In the silence that followed her question, she glanced over her shoulder to find his gaze focused solely on her. "Well?"

"Looks good to me," he said, with an appreciative grin.

Holly rolled her eyes and stepped down from the ladder. "You're supposed to be looking at the tree." She planted her hands on her jean-clad hips and frowned in mock disapproval.

"The tree looks good, too."

Stepping back to admire her handiwork, she adjusted a personalized ornament so their linked names faced outward. "Did you see any more Christmas cards in the mail? I'd like to add them to the streamer." She gestured to the row of cards hanging across one wall.

Clay had to hide a smile. His once-uncluttered penthouse was now a huge curio cabinet for all the knickknacks and mementos Holly had collected over the past two years. "I think there might have been a card or two."

"Well, open them up!" Holly scooted the stepladder over to the wall and began sliding the cards aside to make more room.

He tore open a bright green envelope and pulled out the card. "It's from Anne." He laughed. "She says since Mother was so impressed by your Christmas dinner last year, we get to host the family again."

"If I had known that, I would have let you cook." Holly smirked.

"Oh, very funny." He slid open another envelope. "Burn the hamburgers at one Fourth of July picnic, and you're labeled for life."

"Burn? Incinerate is more like it."

His planned response got caught in his throat as he glanced down at the Christmas photograph card. "Holly, come take a look at this."

Climbing down from the stepladder, she asked, "Is something wrong?"

"No." He handed her the card and carefully watched for her reaction.

The card trembled slightly in her hand. She traced a fingertip over the glossy photo of Lucas seated in Santa's lap. A huge smile lit the little boy's face. "Look how big he's getting! I can't believe he's in kindergarten already."

A short letter accompanied the card, and Clay skimmed it quickly. "His grandmother says he loves school, and he wants to play T-ball in the spring."

"He'll have so much fun." Holly held the card against her chest. Her eyes were suspiciously bright as she said, "You know, I think this deserves the place of honor."

He smiled tenderly. "The refrigerator?" he asked.

Holly nodded and carried the card into the kitchen. She had to rearrange a few of Lucas's recent paintings and other pictures to make room. The childish artwork and photographs formed a collage that chronicled the time Lucas had spent at Hopewell House and with them, and also the past two years, during which he'd lived with his grandmother.

"We're going to need another refrigerator," Clay teased, wrapping his arms around her and drawing her back against his chest.

Holly glanced over her shoulder and smiled. "I think you're right." Turning in his embrace, she rose up to kiss him quickly. She took his hand and led him back into the living room. "Come here. I want to show you something."

Together they knelt down in front of the Christmas tree, and he laughed as she sorted through the presents. "Holly, Christmas is still two weeks away!" He hadn't even done all his shopping yet. "I thought our tradition was to open one gift the night before."

"I know!" She found the present she was looking for and held it out to him. Excited color tinted her cheeks. "But I can't wait."

The lightweight present was the size of a small shirt box. "Should I try to guess?"

She shook her head, her happiness barely contained in a bright smile. "You'll never get it."

"Then I suppose I'll just have to open it." Clay slid off the ribbon, tore off the paper, and lifted the lid. He brushed aside the tissue paper and stared. Swallowing, he looked up at Holly. His hands shook as he lifted the tiny infant sleeper and baby booties. "Does this mean—"

She nodded before he finished the question. "We're having a baby!" Her words ended in a laugh as he pulled her into his arms amid wrapping paper, ribbons and baby clothes. The excitement she felt at the idea of having Clay's baby was reflected in his blue gaze, and she could hardly wait to see if their child would have his gorgeous eyes.

"Thank you so much for being patient with me," she said. "I know you wanted to try sooner—"

He shook off her gratitude. "I wanted you to be ready. It didn't matter if it was now or years from now."

"How does eight months sound?"

"Eight months sounds perfect. Just perfect." His expression turning serious, he said, "I love you, Holly."

Holly hugged him tightly. "I love you, too," she said against his neck. "Merry Christmas."

He slid his hand between their bodies to embrace her flat stomach. "Well, none of my presents come close to this," he said gruffly.

"That's not true," she said, her eyes shining. "You've already given me the greatest gift of all."

* * * * *

One

Hunter Cabot, Navy SEAL, had a healing bullet wound in his side, thirty days' leave and, apparently, a wife he'd never met.

On the drive into his hometown of Springville, California, he stopped for gas at Charlie Evans's service station. That's where the trouble started.

"Hunter! Man, it's good to see you! Margie didn't tell us you were coming home."

"Margie?" Hunter leaned back against the front fender of his black pickup truck and winced as his side gave a small twinge of pain. Silently then, he watched as the man he'd known since high school filled his tank.

Charlie grinned, shook his head and pumped gas. "Guess your wife was lookin' for a little 'alone' time with you, huh?"

"My—" Hunter couldn't even say the word. *Wife?* He didn't have a wife. "Look, Charlie..."

"Don't blame her, of course," his friend said with a wink as he finished up and put the gas cap back on. "You being gone all the time with the SEALs must be hard on the ol' love life."

He'd never had any complaints, Hunter thought, frowning at the man still talking a mile a minute. "What're you—"

"Bet Margie's anxious to see you. She told us all about that R and R trip you two took to Bali." Charlie's dark brown eyebrows lifted and wiggled.

"Charlie..."

"Hey, it's okay, you don't have to say a thing, man."

What the hell could he say? Hunter shook his head, paid for his gas and as he left, told himself Charlie was just losing it. Maybe the guy had been smelling gas fumes too long.

But as it turned out, it wasn't just Charlie. Stopped at a red light on Main Street, Hunter glanced out his window to smile at Mrs. Harker, his second-grade teacher who was now at least a hundred years old. In the middle of the crosswalk, the old lady stopped and shouted, "Hunter Cabot, you've got yourself a wonderful wife. I hope you appreciate her."

Scowling now, he only nodded at the old woman—the only teacher who'd ever scared the crap out of him. What the hell was going on here? Was everyone but him nuts?

His temper beginning to boil, he put up with a few more comments about his "wife" on the drive through town before finally pulling into the wide, circular drive leading to the Cabot mansion. Hunter didn't have a clue what was going on, but he planned to get to the bottom of it. Fast.

He grabbed his duffel bag, stalked into the house and paid no attention to the housekeeper, who ran at him, fluttering both hands. "Mr. Hunter!"

"Sorry, Sophie," he called out over his shoulder as he took the stairs two at a time. "Need a shower, then we'll talk."

He marched down the long, carpeted hallway to the rooms that were always kept ready for him. In his suite, Hunter tossed the duffel down and stopped dead. The shower in his bathroom was running. His *wife?*

Anger and curiosity boiled in his gut, creating a churning mass that had him moving forward without even thinking about it. He opened the bathroom door to a wall of steam and the sound of a woman singing—off-key. Margie, no doubt.

Well, if she was his wife...Hunter walked across the room, yanked the shower door open and stared in at a curvy, naked, temptingly wet woman.

She whirled to face him, slapping her arms across her naked body while she gave a short, terrified scream.

Hunter smiled. "Hi, honey. I'm home."

* * * * *

Be sure to look for
AN OFFICER AND A MILLIONAIRE
by USA TODAY *bestselling author Maureen Child.*
Available January 2009 from Silhouette Desire.

CELEBRATE
60 YEARS
OF PURE READING PLEASURE
WITH HARLEQUIN®!

We'll be spotlighting a different series every month throughout 2009 to celebrate our 60th anniversary. Look for Silhouette Desire® in January!

Collect all 12 books in the Silhouette Desire® Man of the Month continuity, starting in January 2009 with *An Officer and a Millionaire* by *USA TODAY* bestselling author Maureen Child.

Look for one new Man of the Month title every month in 2009!

Home to Texas and straight to the altar!

Luke: The Cowboy Heir
by
PATRICIA THAYER

Luke never saw himself returning to
Mustang Valley. But as a Randell the land
is in his blood and is calling him back...
And blond beauty Tess Meyers is waiting
for Luke Randell's return....

Available January 2009
wherever you buy books.

www.eHarlequin.com   HR17559

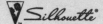

SPECIAL EDITION™

USA TODAY bestselling author
MARIE FERRARELLA

FORTUNES OF TEXAS: RETURN TO RED ROCK

PLAIN JANE AND THE PLAYBOY

To kill time at a New Year's party, playboy Jorge Mendoza shows the host's teenage son how to woo the ladies. The random target of Jorge's charms: wallflower Jane Gilliam. But with one kiss at midnight, introverted Jane turns the tables on this would-be Casanova, as the commitment-phobe falls for her hook, line and sinker!

Available January 2009
wherever you buy books.

Visit Silhouette Books at www.eHarlequin.com   SSE65428

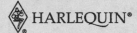

HARLEQUIN®

American ★ *Romance*®

TINA LEONARD
The Texas
Ranger's Twins

Men Made in America

The promise of a million dollars has lured
Texas Ranger Dane Morgan back to his family
ranch. But he can't be forced into marriage to
single mother of twin girls, Suzy Wintertone,
who is tempting as she is sweet—can he?

***Available January 2009
wherever books are sold.***

LOVE, HOME & HAPPINESS

REQUEST YOUR FREE BOOKS!

2 FREE NOVELS PLUS 2 FREE GIFTS!

SPECIAL EDITION®

Life, Love and Family!

YES! Please send me 2 FREE Silhouette Special Edition® novels and my 2 FREE gifts (gifts are worth about $10). After receiving them, if I don't wish to receive any more books, I can return the shipping statement marked "cancel." If I don't cancel, I will receive 6 brand-new novels every month and be billed just $4.24 per book in the U.S. or $4.99 per book in Canada, plus 25¢ shipping and handling per book and applicable taxes, if any*. That's a savings of at least 15% off the cover price! I understand that accepting the 2 free books and gifts places me under no obligation to buy anything. I can always return a shipment and cancel at any time. Even if I never buy another book from Silhouette, the two free books and gifts are mine to keep forever.

235 SDN EEYU 335 SDN EEY6

Name	(PLEASE PRINT)	
Address		Apt. #
City	State/Prov.	Zip/Postal Code

Signature (if under 18, a parent or guardian must sign)

Mail to the **Silhouette Reader Service:**
IN U.S.A.: P.O. Box 1867, Buffalo, NY 14240-1867
IN CANADA: P.O. Box 609, Fort Erie, Ontario L2A 5X3

Not valid to current subscribers of Silhouette Special Edition books.

Want to try two free books from another line?
Call 1-800-873-8635 or visit www.morefreebooks.com.

* Terms and prices subject to change without notice. N.Y. residents add applicable sales tax. Canadian residents will be charged applicable provincial taxes and GST. Offer not valid in Quebec. This offer is limited to one order per household. All orders subject to approval. Credit or debit balances in a customer's account(s) may be offset by any other outstanding balance owed by or to the customer. Please allow 4 to 6 weeks for delivery. Offer available while quantities last.

Your Privacy: Silhouette is committed to protecting your privacy. Our Privacy Policy is available online at www.eHarlequin.com or upon request from the Reader Service. From time to time we make our lists of customers available to reputable third parties who may have a product or service of interest to you. If you would prefer we not share your name and address, please check here. ☐

 Silhouette®

COMING NEXT MONTH

SPECIAL EDITION

#1945 THE STRANGER AND TESSA JONES—
Christine Rimmer
Bravo Family Ties

The Bravos meet the Jones Gang as two of Christine Rimmer's famous Special Edition families come together in one very special book. Snowed in with an amnesiac stranger during a freak blizzard, Tessa Jones soon finds out her guest is none other than heartbreaker Ash Bravo. And that's when things really heat up....

#1946 PLAIN JANE AND THE PLAYBOY—Marie Ferrarella
Fortunes of Texas: Return to Red Rock

To kill time at a New Year's party, playboy Jorge Mendoza shows the host's teenage son how to woo the ladies. The random target of Jorge's charms: wallflower Jane Gilliam. But with one kiss at midnight, introverted Jane turns the tables on this would-be Casanova, as the commitment-phobe falls for her hook, line and sinker!

#1947 COWBOY TO THE RESCUE—Stella Bagwell
Men of the West

Hired to investigate the mysterious death of the Sandbur Ranch matriarch's late husband, private investigator Christina Logan enlists the help of cowboy-to-the-core Lex Saddler, Sandbur's youngest—and singlest—scion. Together, they find the truth...and each other.

#1948 REINING IN THE RANCHER—Karen Templeton
Wed in the West

Horse breeder Johnny Griego is blindsided by the news—both his ex-girlfriend Thea Benedict *and* his teenage daughter are pregnant. Never one to shirk responsibility, Johnny does the right thing and proposes to Thea. But Thea wants happily-ever-after, not a mere marriage of convenience. Can she rein in the rancher enough to have both?

#1949 SINGLE MOM SEEKS...—Teresa Hill

All newly divorced Lily Tanner wants is a safe, happy life with her two adorable daughters. Until hunky FBI agent Nick Malone moves in next door with his orphaned nephew. Now the pretty single mom's single days just might be numbered....

#1950 I STILL DO—Christie Ridgway

During a chance reunion in Vegas, former childhood sweethearts Will Dailey and Emily Garner let loose a little and make good on an old pledge—to wed each other if they weren't otherwise taken by age thirty! But in the cold light of day, the firefighter and librarian's quickie marriage doesn't seem like such a bright idea. Would their whim last a lifetime?

SSECNM1208BPA